SHERLOCK HOLMES: ZOMBIES OVER LONDON

STEPHEN MERTZ

DARK WOLF BOOKS

Sherlock Holmes: Zombies Over London
Kindle Edition
Copyright © 2025 (As Revised) by Stephen Mertz

Dark Wolf Books
An Imprint of Wolfpack Publishing
1707 E. Diana Street
Tampa, FL 33610

www.darkwolfbooks.com

Paperback ISBN 979-8-89567-932-6
Ebook ISBN 979-8-89567-939-5

For David Avallone, Noonman incarnate, who knows a hero when he sees one.

SHERLOCK HOLMES: ZOMBIES OVER LONDON

From the Journal
of
Dr. John H. Watson

CHAPTER 1

The steady thrum of steam engines shivered through the enormous military dirigible *Blackhawk*, belying the high rate of speed at which we cut through the night sky.

I stood in the angle of one of the huge braces that lined the walls and watched Commander Standish complete the adjustments on the "flight enabler" strapped to Sherlock Holmes' back. With its metal framework, the fabric draping between the struts floated about Holmes like a cloak.

Standish turned to me.

"Your turn, Doctor."

He worked the frame over my shoulders and buckled the straps.

We rode in a small anteroom along the outer shell of the airship, well aft of the control and radio rooms. A large portal opened in the anteroom's side. Brisk air rushed in around us, and though I stood well away from the edge, I could see the winking lights of Devonshire spread out below.

Then, so suddenly that it was like entering a portal to another world, the thrum of the engines simply stopped. The great ship glided along the lower edge of the clouds, cutting them silently.

Holmes nodded with satisfaction and, gripping the framework of the great door, leaned out into the darkness.

"Right on time," he said. "And there – do you see it, Watson?"

I said, "I *feel* it!"

Below and off to the right the walls of Castle Moriarity rose, thick and impenetrable, like the bones of some great, fossilized beast jutting from the stony ground. I stepped to the portal, steadied myself, and leaned out slightly, taking in the approaching lights. I had not grown accustomed to the utter silence, and without the vibration of the engines, the swiftness of our flight had an eerie, disorienting effect.

The *Blackhawk* was magnificent. Developed in secret, the dirigible had been housed in the shell of an industrial complex north of London. Based on an original design stolen by British agents from the files of Ferdinand von Zeppelin more than a decade earlier, *Blackhawk* was nothing less than a manifestation of the future. The first time I saw her, tethered to a stone and metal tower deep inside that hangar, her streamlined shape and stark black tail had given her the aspect of a tethered behemoth, transported from a far planet.

Blackhawk's long, ominous shape was a formidable, nearly invisible presence moving silently through darkness. The outer envelope of the airship concealed huge cells that contained a lighter than air gas. Forward thrust was provided by engines, mounted in cowlings, of a type previously only imagined existing in the dreams of madmen, or dreamers like Jules Verne. In that year of grace, 1895, on the ground below, the world went on about its business as it always had. Steam power waged war with horse-drawn carriages, weapons grew ever more complex and powerful, and here, far above it all, a new world was being forged.

It has occurred to me, in my efforts to chronicle the exploits of Mr. Sherlock Holmes, that I have perhaps too often acquiesced to my friend's desire that such accounts focus on his unique cognitive abilities. Holmes is, of course, correct in priding himself in those powers of deduction and reasoning which constitute his discipline, and yet I have always been of the opinion that equal attention should be paid to the remarkable warrior he could become, a formidable opponent in nearly every form of combat.

Our plan was a simple one. Holmes and I, clad all in black, would leap from the doorway of this amazing ship. We would be invisible against the night sky. We would glide down with the grace of descending birds and light inside the castle walls. That was the plan.

A plan of which I was not altogether enthusiastic.

"Ready, Watson?" Holmes' query crackled with enthusiasm.

I gestured with my arms in a mildly exaggerated flapping motion. The lightweight material fluttered.

"I'd be a damn sight more ready if this contraption of yours had been field tested at least once before I have to depend on it while I step into thin air like a man leaping off a bridge."

"Courage, Watson." The chiding was softened with the twitch of a grin. "You were a combat surgeon in Afghanistan. You've faced death before."

"True enough, and I'd step into the pits of Hell to take on Lucifer himself if it meant saving Mary."

A shadow emerged from a corner of the cabin.

Normally I might have been startled or aggravated but at the moment, with everything else that was going on, the appearance of Mycroft Holmes, Sherlock Holmes' brother, did somehow not come a complete surprise.

"Good Doctor Watson, you *will* be stepping into Hell down there, and we *are* taking on Lucifer's premier ambassador here on earth. With your wife held hostage by Moriarty, I would much prefer that you and my dear brother would allow a squad of able-bodied men to accompany you."

I said, "Absolutely not. An overt assault of any kind would only result in Mary's death."

He said, "A singular sequence of events has placed each of us in the predicament in which we now find ourselves. And so, you and my brother will leap to your deaths, one way or another, and I am unable to dissuade you of this suicide mission you've undertaken?"

Holmes registered no surprise. "And how long have you been monitoring the activities of Doctor Watson and me, dear brother?" There was an acidic tone to my friend's voice. His eyes were glacial, his demeanor petulant.

Mycroft Holmes was seven years his brother's senior. There was a vague resemblance notable in their facial structure, but Mycroft was a much stouter and larger man than my friend. Heavily built and massive, he had the high brow of an intellectual and alert, steel gray eyes of an interrogation specialist. In fact, he was both at the time of which I write. Mycroft Holmes was Her Majesty's Chief of Intelligence. As our nation's top intelligence officer (a fact known to only a few people at that time, I should add), Mycroft had most recently exerted himself on our behalf in the matter I chronicled under the heading of "The Adventure of the Bruce-Partington Plans."

Despite their late middle age, there was a sibling rivalry between these two that surely had its roots in childhood, yet in adulthood, it wore the cold mask of icy impersonality when matters not familial were being discussed.

Mycroft said, "One of my agents picked up the scent at Lady Fairfax's dinner party."

"Of course," said Holmes. "The waiter, overly solicitous of our end of the table."

"He's been in place in the household staff for some time. Naturally, he recognized you."

"That dinner party was only the beginning," said Holmes. "Lady Fairfax's nephew is a German spy. Count Kleinhart was at that dinner party to meet someone."

I listened to the brothers address each other as if in a verbal match to best one another which, I had come to learn, was their standard form of verbal communication.

Outside, the lights of Castle Moriarty drew closer in the darkness below. It had indeed been a circuitous and yet, time-wise, compressed chain of events that had taken Holmes and me from Lady Fairfax's sumptuous dinner party in London to us four in this enclosed windy dark space aboard the gondola of a midnight black dirigible.

The trail of clues, subtle at first, began at that dinner party and interested Holmes to the extent he had undertaken a private investigation into Count Kleinhart, utilizing his own resources, moti-vated as far as I could discern mainly by a distinct dislike of the man's supercilious manner. Though subtle, the clues had not long challenged Holmes' powers of ratiocination. He sensed the hand of Moriarty at work behind the scenes as a pure-bred hunting dog picks up that first faint scent of the fox.

Holmes and I were on the trail of something the extent of which we could not guess and did not yet know. One thing alone became increasingly apparent. Professor Moriarty had devised some evil scheme or service that he was auctioning off to the highest bidder among the European monarchies. Kleinhart represented interests in Germany that wished to acquire whatever Moriarty was selling. And the closer we got to learning the nature of that scheme or service, the more dangerous the "game" became.

There had thus far been three narrow escapes from death. A falling ton brick from a construction site we'd been walking past. A racing brougham rattling down a narrow cobblestone street. Only the fortuitous presence of the mouth of an alley that we dived into saved our lives that time. Someone had taken a shot at us as we were leaving our apartment in Baker Street. None of these deterred us, which is why the blackguards struck closer to home.

They kidnapped my wife.

The warning was clear enough.

Desist or Mary dies!

Mary would not expect me to cower, to back off. I'd experienced combat as a soldier. I'd shared some narrow escapes with Holmes. Nothing but death itself would stop me from rescuing her.

Holmes' final deduction in the matter, similar

cigar ash found in two locations, established the guilt of a prominent financier who, under threat of exposure, provided the final piece of the puzzle that led us to determine that Castle Moriarty was where my Mary was being held.

Commander Standish leaned away from staring out into the blackness. "We're passing over the castle now, Mr. Holmes."

Holmes stepped forward, bracing himself in the doorway of the cabin. His hair and clothing flapped in the wind. "Remember, Watson, what I told you about aerodynamic control."

I joined him at the doorway. "I'll do my best," was the best I could muster.

Mycroft rested a heavy hand on each of our shoulders. "I want to thank you both on behalf of Her Majesty's Government. Given that a troublemaker like Count Kleinhart would express interest in whatever Moriarty has up for sale, it becomes imperative, in the name of national security, that we learn what the Professor is up to in that accursed castle of his."

Holmes said, with a perfectly straight face except for the merest hint of a smile, "Gentlemen, it is time to test my invention."

Before Mycroft, Standish, or I could voice any reply, Holmes stepped through the doorway as if walking from one room to another, leaving me no alternative but to send Standish and Mycroft a parting glance.

I then took a deep breath and stepped out into empty space.

CHAPTER 2

I was airborne.

The night enveloped me as I dropped like a rock away from the airship that was already invisible above us except where its giant, long shape blotted out the stars. I started picking up speed, plummeting down, down, down, the air rushing by me, whipping at my hair and clothes. The lights of the castle were racing up toward me.

The *Blackhawk* would be banking away. I had lost sight of Holmes. I was on my own, hoping to bloody blazes that Holmes' invention was working and that my companion was not already lying crushed, broken and dead somewhere down on the dark ground. Two bloody fools crazy enough to jump out of a dirigible that wasn't supposed to exist! As instructed, I raised my arms out from my side after having counted to seven, then breathed a mighty sigh of relief when I felt the chest harness tighten as the fabric grew taut, considerably lessening my rate of descent. The wind was cold, whistling.

For the briefest span of time, my soul yielded to such a liberating sense of freedom as I have never known except in dreams. I was flying! The sensation was spectacular and filled me with an urge to shout, but of course, that was an impulse I denied.

Less than sixty seconds later, I was guiding myself into a running stop upon the roof of the castle, stopping just short of charging full force into the stone parapets under the momentum of my landing. I dug in my heels.

First order of business was to shed the unique harness, which was accomplished with a loosening of the quick-release clips Holmes had devised. I drew my Webley revolver, my eyes darting across the castle rooftop, my night vision having adequately adjusted during my descent.

Holmes crouched on one knee beyond a stone structure that framed stairs leading down into the building, his pistol drawn, concealing himself behind one of the parapets, observing something through a pair of miniature binoculars. His lean frame was limned in a vague golden glow of illumination from below.

Relief coursed through me with the knowledge that we had survived the "field test" of his invention for leaping out of dirigibles. I rushed to join him.

Engrossed as he was, he did not draw his eyes from the binoculars but rather acknowledged my presence with a curt, "I see you've made it, Watson. Good. We have our work cut out for us."

I crouched next to him, producing and snapping open my set of binoculars to see what so keenly held his interest.

A courtyard, three stories below our position, bustled with activity in flickering torch and lamplight. The courtyard was bordered on one side by the main structure, opposite which was a main front gate set in a high stone wall that encompassed the castle grounds. Beyond the wide-open wrought iron gates, a narrow road snaked off into the gloom of the surrounding countryside. A long, low garage with closed doors and a storehouse faced a row of barracks. The activity centered around a pair of horse-drawn wagons that stood beside the loading dock of the storage warehouse.

The wagons were being methodically loaded with an assortment of boxes and crates.

The boxed cargo being loaded, which could have been anything from scientific equipment to household items, was not what arrested my attention. Rather, I was struck with the peculiar manner in which the workers went about transporting the crates from the building to the wagons. Their movements were *too* methodical, *too* precise. They ambulated without speaking, which could have been under instruction, certainly, yet there was about the workers a uniform rigidity of demeanor, a precise cadence to each and every movement and a peculiar similarity of physical appearance.

The men and women, I counted fifteen of them, appeared to be of a uniform age, approximately thirty I would estimate. Light poured from the doorway of the warehouse, through which each of them passed, thus forming one continuous line that afforded me an unobstructed glimpse of each. They wore matching threadbare clothing, the men in gray work shirts and trousers, the women in shifts.

Several men, armed with rifles, formed a loose semi-circle around the loading dock, keeping what I sensed, even from our vantage point, a wary eye on the shuffling figures who went about their work like sleepwalkers, their arms hanging limply at their sides when they weren't carrying the boxes. Their expressions were blank and empty-eyed.

"Holmes, what in God's name--?"

"Zombies." He snapped shut the binoculars and returned them to the pouch at his hip. "The undead."

I studied him in the faint light, trying unsuccessfully to detect some hint of a mild jest.

"Bosh. That's superstition, like werewolves and vampires."

"Hardly." Holmes' tone of voice was authoritative. "Unlike those superstitious you cite, there is, in fact, a scientific basis for—"

"All right, all right." I could not abide my friend's pedantic nature while my heart hammered against my ribs like a kettle drum. I continued to scan the wagons, the loading dock, and those strange figures moving about. "What about my Mary?"

He pointed away from the loading dock, to the inky gloom near the front gate. "There, Watson."

I cursed myself for having been overly focused on the loading dock and the strange figures there. My blood was running hot, but as always, the cool analytical eye of my friend had observed something barely visible unless you stared hard at an area against the wall.

The form of a coach. A horse. A driver.

And there she was! My breath caught in my throat.

"Good heavens! Those... *things* have her."

My heartbeat increased, the blood pounding in my ears. I held my pistol so tightly, I feared I might crush the grip.

Mary stood between two of what Holmes had called zombies. Two of the hulking male figures each gripped one of her arms above the elbow. And with my outrage there stormed through me a surge of pride, for Mary did not cower despite their towering hulks looming above her.

My Mary was trim of figure, well-dressed in crinoline. She stood with her back ramrod straight and her chin lifted.

I whispered to Holmes, "We must get to her. We must formulate a plan."

"Of course, dear fellow. Observe more closely."

I was irritated and impatient in equal measure, yet I sharpened the focus of the binoculars to see if I could make out more down there where the coach stood near the front gate, away from the loading dock. I made out some indefinite shadow down there that was more of an impression than something tangible. I held my breath.

The strange, shambling figures were now engaged in securing tarps over the crates on the wagons.

The man with the lantern was crossing the courtyard to confer with someone, who stood by the coach near Mary and the pair of brutes who had her in their grasp. When the amber glow of the lantern reached the coach, I had a sudden good look at the man who was obviously in charge here. The man Holmes and I had risked our lives to track down.

Moriarty was tall and thin, and white-haired. His solemn, ascetic appearance and aloof manner emanated disdain just as the constant swinging of his head from side to side, like a snake ready to strike, bespoke a cunning alertness that, with his ruthlessness, was the dominating force in his rise to the apex of crime in London. A malevolent evil shimmered like an aura around the man. He dismissed the underling who withdrew, leaving Moriarty again in complete darkness.

"But how do we get down there?" I whispered. "The castle must be thick with Moriarty's minions."

"Not necessarily. Whatever he's up to, Professor Moriarty exhibits extreme concern over his work remaining secret. Why else here, in such a remote area? We have three advantages. Surprise and stealth."

"That's two."

"Observe, Watson. Deduce."

"I already have. Moriarty must know his game is up, at least as far as this location goes. He's withdrawing."

Holmes pocketed his binoculars.

I was bristling for action. I could see no activity beyond where Moriarty waited with my Mary and the loading dock where the human hulks stood passively in a group, their task complete. The garage remained dark; its doors closed. No indication of activity stirred in the dark, massive castle beneath us.

I said, "Let's go."

I bolted for the stairs,

Holmes was right behind me.

CHAPTER 3

We made our way down to the ground level of the castle. Faint lamplight illuminated the landings of the wide staircases down which we ran.

It was a chilly, stagnant, tomb-like place of stone walls and stone floors. Dank, as if untouched by the warmth of day or by life itself. We encountered no one during our hurried descent. I had the weirdest sensation that the house was a slumbering giant around us, a malignant organism, ancient and yet possessing a potent evil.

Holmes and I slowed our pace as we crossed a grand reception chamber and came to tall double oak front doors that had been left yawning wide, opening onto the courtyard. We advanced on the doorway from separate angles of approach, crouching to its either side, our weapons drawn. We peered into the courtyard.

The scene by the coach had not much changed in

the brief passage of time that it had taken Holmes and me to make our way down from the castle roof. The figures of the hulking brutes with their grip on Mary's arms, her defiant posture, the waiting coach and the black horses scratching the earth with impatient hooves were clearly etched in the light from the loading dock.

Moriarty no longer stood beside the coach. He was now at a point halfway between it and the loading dock. He stood with his hands clasped behind his back as he conferred with an overseer.

The dreadful beings now stood passively clustered near the loading dock, men and women blank of eye and expressionless, arms hanging at their sides.

I gauged the short distance from the coach to the open front gateway in the stone wall. I gauged the distance from our position to where the hulking forms stood near Mary.

I pitched my voice low. "Holmes, it's perfect. Which one do you want, right or left?"

He knew I was talking about the brutes, but his attention was on Moriarty.

"It's a shame to leave him. A shame to leave him alive."

"Holmes, I know you have a score to settle, but right now our only priority is getting Mary out of this hell hole. Nothing else matters, so do kindly get that through your blasted analytical skull." I holstered the Webley. "I'm going for the one on the right. A tackle from his blind side should take him down."

Holmes holstered his pistol.

"Right you are. The one on the left is mine."

As if we had rehearsed the maneuver a dozen times, we quit the veranda and sprinted noiselessly through the darkness. In perfect tandem, we launched into flying tackles intended to take down the brutes.

It was like hurling myself against the trunk of a tree! I had gained considerable momentum in the sprint from the doorway, and I impacted with considerable force. Enough force to practically crush my shoulders upon impact and wrench my neck with a dulling of the senses.

I rolled away with an unbidden groan of pain and frustration.

The brutes emitted slow-witted sounds of reaction, uttering "Huh?" in unison. They released Mary.

She did not run! When she saw me, her lovely face came alive.

"John!"

Each of these dead-eyed monsters moved with surprising speed and yet with no indication of exertion or remark of any kind. One of them leaped for me while the other went for Holmes.

Extended arms groped for my throat. There was a rank stench to the fellow. A chill emanated from him, as if he were dead. I managed to draw my revolver as his momentum took me down and he fell atop me, a dead weight with his cold fingers clasping my throat. I heard a thrashing upon the ground nearby from the direction where Holmes had been taken down.

Mary gasped, but she did not scream and even at such a moment I admired the pure spunk and cool-headedness of the woman I loved.

But most of my senses started darkening around the edges, my breath coming in panting gasps as frigid leathery thumbs tightened around my larynx. Fetid breath spewed from his mouth that was a black O in his dead-eyed face, inches from my own. The world began to swim around me from lack of oxygen.

I managed to bring up the Webley, place its barrel through the O of his mouth and pull the trigger three times. The brute reared back and I scampered to escape his clutches. He roared a blood-lust cry even with a third of his skull blown away before pitching backwards to become an unmoving heap.

I sprang to my feet. My first glance was in Mary's direction.

She stood there, her back remaining ramrod straight but one hand clenched to her widened mouth to stem a reflexive scream while her other arm extended, pointing at where the second brute had pinned Holmes to the ground.

I dashed forward to help my friend, who struggled valiantly but in vain against the dominant force of the fiend whose animated strength seemed unstoppable. Holmes had unholstered his revolver but the zombie (I could now think of these beings as nothing else) had one of his mighty hands around Holmes' throat, choking my companion just as I had been strangled, while the other arm pinned down the wrist of Holmes' hand that gripped his gun. I reached them. I placed the muzzle of my revolver against the zombie's forehead and pulled the trigger three times, effectively blowing the thing's head off his shoulder, the skull disintegrating into a bloody splash. I lifted a boot and kicked the headless form so that it would not fall upon Holmes. I rapidly reloaded my revolver.

Holmes rose unsteadily, massaging his throat. "Thank you, old cock." His voice rattled like stones in a tin cup even as the keen alertness returned to his steely eyes.

I said, "I rather think of myself as a mother hen."

Then my arms were filled with Mary, who dashed into them. Exhilaration coursed through me.

Mary was breathing heavily from exertion and stress. "John, my darling! I somehow knew you'd come for me. I never doubted that you and Mrs. Holmes would come for me!"

Her beauty! Her firm young body held in my embrace! Her determined, fighting spirit that had never admitted defeat! This was a woman worth charging into the pits of hell for!

In the coolness of the night air, her breath was warm and arousing against my neck. I could not resist. I leaned down and we traded the briefest kiss that was moist and vibrant with promise and eroticism.

Holmes spoke sharply. "Watson!"

I whirled to see what he was referring to without releasing my embrace of Mary's trim waist.

The remaining zombies were advancing across the courtyard in our direction, their arms extended with fingers clutched like talons, advancing at a considerable rate of speed despite their vacant eyes and shuffling gait,

There was no sign of Moriarty or his overseer. They had vanished from sight behind the closing ranks of advancing zombies, which drew ever closer.

It was eerie how silent they were save for the shuffling of their feet. They were close enough now that their collective stench filled the nostrils, taking me back momentarily to the Afghan killing field of my military years. After a battle, the enemy corpses would lie unclaimed to rot in the sun.

Mary screamed.

I lifted my revolver and squeezed off a couple of rounds. Body shots. I could hear the *thunk* of bullets striking flesh. I could hear the splatter of the exit wounds from their backs. But they kept on coming.

Holmes said, "The living dead. Only head shots will stop them, Watson, nothing else. Damn! Where is Moriarty?"

I holstered my revolver and swept Mary off her feet, into my arms. "We have what we came for. It's time for a strategic withdrawal." I hurried toward the coach, holding her in my arms.

I said to Holmes, Holmes said, "Quite so."

He leaped onto the coach seat where the driver, a young fellow with a lantern jaw, stood gaping at this abrupt upheaval of events. Holmes clipped him with a stiff and efficiently delivered right to the jaw. The unconscious driver disappeared over the opposite side of the coach.

Holmes took hold of the reins. The side door of the coach was open for Moriarty, but instead, I started to place Mary inside. The zombies who were now no more than a dozen paces from us, almost upon us.

A shot rang out.

Mary said, *"Oh!"* in a small voice.

She went limp in my arms.

CHAPTER 4

A trace of scarlet lined Mary's skin just beneath the tangle of curls. I set her inside the coach, again drawing my revolver. I only caught a fleeting glimpse of Moriarty before he was again blocked from view by the oncoming zombies.

Holmes said, "Hang on, Watson."

The snap of the horsewhip cracked like a gunshot.

I leapt aboard the coach just in time for the bone-jarring jolt of the forward motion that packed enough kick to snap the door shut after me. I wrapped my arms around Mary. My heart skipped a beat and my throat went dry when her head lulled unconsciously against my shoulder. I brushed aside tendrils of her hair and then brushed away the scarlet ribbon where the bullet had grazed her left temple. I lowered my ear to her nostrils but could discern nothing.

Holmes expertly worked the reins. We raced through the front gate. I managed to lean out through the window for a backward glance. The zombies mulled aimlessly around where the coach had been moments earlier. Along one side of the courtyard, the doors of the long, low garage were rising in mechanized unison. Then the coach was skidding into a two-wheeled turn.

I held Mary close, hugging her so that my body cushioned the jostling of the coach as it righted itself, the wheels struggling to gain traction, spewing dirt before clattering down a narrow, winding road that snaked into the night. I again craned my neck out through the open window.

A trio of strange, over-sized motor carriages came bolting through the castle's front gate in hot pursuit, huge motor carriages powered by massive steam engines whose unleashed fury pummeled the night even more loudly than the galloping hoof beats. Unusually bright headlamps pierced the night like silver daggers. They effortlessly negotiated the treacherous terrain, closing in on us as soon as they burst into view. They were top-heavy with men waving rifles. Moriarty's armed guard!

I had to narrow my eyes and squint to make sure I was seeing what came next because it happened too fast for me to reach for my binoculars. A small version of the impressive steam-powered motor carriages suddenly shot through the open gate in the castle wall but did not follow the others in pursuit of us. This lone, smaller contraption gained speed as it angled away in the opposite direction, undoubtedly carrying Professor Moriarty. I had to blink because I could not believe what I saw considering the distance and the night. It appeared to be speeding along without wheels of any kind touching the ground, suspended slightly above the ground!

It rocketed off and disappeared.

Gunfire winked red from the gaining steam-powered carriages. Two, three, four angry hornets spat through the interior of the coach, and more could be heard whistling through the darkness outside.

From his perch atop the racing coach, Holmes shouted down, "It looks as if we may have had it!"

I tried drawing a bead on the closest headlamp. "I'll see what I can do!"

Mary stirred. I peered into her hazed but steadfast eyes.

"Thank God, Mary! I was afraid you'd been--"

She grasped our situation through the mental haze reflected in her eyes. She saw the revolver in my hand.

"I'm all right, John. Do what you must."

From on high came Holmes' voice.

"Watson!"

I leaned out again through the window, doing my best to draw a bead on one of those glaring headlamps. I squeezed off a round that had no appreciable effect except for inciting a renewed volley of gunfire from the men riding aboard those machines. The report of my handgun sounded inconsequential against the thundering clatter of the racing coach and the heavy fire from those strange contraptions, now less than a quarter mile behind us.

The castle had receded from sight beyond folds in the forbidding terrain so that only those infernal headlamps provided respite against the utter blackness of night. Our horses would be thundering along the snaking road from instinct while headlights allowed the steam engine carriages to chase us three abreast, easily negotiating boulders and dips in the terrain even as they gained speed.

I pulled off another shot, and this time one of the three headlamps went dark.

Startled, panicky shouts carried from that machine, that's how close they were. Then in the illumination of the other headlamps, the darkened machine hit something that made it into a somersaulting mass of crunching metal. Airborne bodies tumbled everywhere.

The other drivers swerved around the wreckage and continued after us. The gunfire from those machines resumed, and suddenly my revolver was struck by a lucky bullet. The Webley flew from my hand, which felt like it was being stung by needles.

Alarm animated Mary's features.

"Darling, are you all right?"

I shook my hand, feeling sensation return.

"No, but I am unarmed. I must join Holmes

topside. He has a gun. I can fire on them from atop the coach while he—"

A strange whistling—loud, unearthly—sent a shock of recognition through my system and I was back on the battlefront again.

Mary said, "John, what--?"

Reflex took over.

"Incoming!"

I wrapped my arms about her once again, this time to shield her from what could only be a bomb-shell about to explode, though I well knew that my shielding her would not do either of us much good if that incoming shell scored a direct hit on the carriage.

The explosion, when it came, was near enough to reverberate with a harsh gold flash that for a moment enveloped us. But the coach was spared. A near miss?

The gunfire tapered off from the pursuing steam-powered machines. I peered out. Another of them had taken the hit and become a rolling ball of fire that stopped rolling when it collided with an outcrop of rock.

Then the keening whistle sound again and the remaining machine and those in it were obliterated in another explosion of flame and thunder. This explosion was close enough to send shrapnel and debris raining down upon our coach.

It took Holmes nearly a quarter mile to rein in the panicky steeds drawing our coach. The poor animals had been scared out of their wits, but finally, we drifted to a stop.

Holmes leaped down, concern etched into his lean features.

"Watson, is Mary—?"

Mary responded in a weak voice. "I'll be quite all right, Mr. Holmes. I just feel a little... lightheaded."

I started to speak but my words were drowned out as a line of cavalrymen appeared out of nowhere, uniformed British cavalrymen who stormed past us at a full gallop, vibrating the ground beneath our feet.

Commander Standish brought up the rear, astride a black charger that lifted its front lefts and whinnied.

Holmes was in high spirits.

"You see, Watson! As your dime novel colleagues of the American colonies would have it, we are saved by the cavalry! Hullo, Commander!"

Standish remained in the saddle, surveying the flames in the distance toward which his men rode.

"You didn't think I was going to leave you behind, did you, gentlemen? Yours was an audacious plan, Mr. Holmes, but it never hurts to have backup."

"I heartily agree," said Holmes. "My regards, Commander, to your artillerymen."

I stepped down from the coach. When Mary took the arm I extended to assist her, I gave a tug and then stooped to catch her when she tipped forward, off-balance with a gasp of surprise. I held her in my arms. She rested her wild tangle of curls against my chest with an exhausted but contented sigh.

I said, "Mary has sustained what appears to be a slight wound. No immediate danger but I didn't want to take any chances. We must get her to the nearest hospital."

The Commander nodded. Under ordinary circumstances that would require considerable travel, given our present remote location. However, I daresay this night has hardly been one of ordinary circumstance, eh?"

The starlight behind him disappeared as the *Blackhawk* appeared with its flight lights on, an enormous presence hovering at treetop level. A wicker basket was lowered by a rope.

Holmes and Standish assisted me in lifting and placing Mary's semi-conscious form into the basket.

Holmes said to Standish, "Moriarty."

"I have men after him, Mr. Holmes. "If he left a trail, my chaps will find it right enough."

We stepped back from the basket. I gave the rope a tug. The basket started to rise.

Holmes showed little interest in this. He looked about.

"And my brother?"

Standish said, "Mr. Mycroft Holmes was called to Number Ten Downing Street on a matter of urgency. I'm afraid that's all I know."

"Of course, Commander." Holmes nodded. "Matters of state always take precedence in my brother's life."

I wondered if anyone else present detected the faintest trace of disappointment that I heard in that remark.

Overhead, the *Blackhawk* was lowering the wicker basket for its next boarder.

CHAPTER 5

"You're quite right," said Holmes one month later. "Your readers may be gullible enough to want to read about zombies but no editor who fancies himself a man of the world would buy one syllable of it."

These were the first words to pass between us in thirty minutes.

It was a close, rainy day in March. I sat in my favorite chair and had idled the past thirty minutes lost in thought, gazing through the rain-streaked window at what few pedestrians and carriages sought to brave the inclement weather that made the world a gloomy place.

I said with a chuckle, "Holmes, for you to draw such a 'deduction,' based on my prolonged reflection, is frankly beneath you. Has there been a day since our return to London from Devonshire that one or both of us has not raised the matter of what happened there, of Moriarty's escape?"

He stood before the mantle of the little sitting room of 221B Baker Street and set his beloved violin in its case. He sat down and lit his pipe.

Holmes, Mary, and I had been debriefed by Commander Standish. From Mycroft, there had been no further communication, which was normal given what I knew of relations between the Holmes brothers. Mycroft would be hard at work at the Ministry or buried deep in his seclusion within the Diogenes Club.

Mary had fully recovered from her wound; a stalwart creature of beauty, grace, and intellect, and now I knew her mettle. She and her mother were presently away at the seashore, visiting a relative whose health was in decline. I had already posted my daily missive to her that morning and had received and read her letter to me.

Holmes had lapsed into that peculiar ennui that often gripped him between cases. I had seen no indication that he had resumed his recreational use of cocaine, a habit I frowned on as I was well aware of the drug's ultimately debilitating effect on the mind and body.

On this morning, however, Holmes' playing of Mendelssohn seemed to have lifted his spirit.

And I will admit that at the moment of his remark, my thoughts indeed were centered on precisely how to convey through prose those events that had transpired at Castle Moriarty.

"Each day you begin composing upon a fresh, crisp new sheet of paper," said he. "You then cease writing approximately midway down the third page. The muse is a difficult mistress, is she not?"

I sighed my frustration.

"I can hardly break the oath of secrecy I pledged both you personally and Her Majesty's government. And by the way, it is considered a breach of common etiquette to read over someone's shoulder."

"I was not reading, dear fellow, I was glancing." He tapped out a bowl of ash from his pipe. "Common etiquette has never been my strong suit. My advice is to leave the matter unchronicled."

"I regret to say that I've reached the same conclusion," I admitted. "It's simply not feasible to contribute such a lurid and singular episode to a canon of work which has thus far maintained a modicum of good taste."

"If not restraint," Holmes muttered under his breath. He tapped down a fresh bowl of his imported tobacco. "But you believe, don't you, Watson?"

"I was there. I saw those walking abominations doing Moriarty's bidding. I've read the texts you've called to my attention. In voodoo patois, the Professor is their *bokor* and they the living dead, under his sorcerer's control because they have no will of their own. It's the scientific data that's compelling. The appropriate drugs entered into the bloodstream as a powder, *the coup de poudre*, and a living person becomes a zombie. That is Moriarty's hold over those poor devils. Holmes, what in God's name could he be up to with those... *zombies*?"

His countenance became as gloomy as the weather outside our window. "When I know that, Watson, my life will again attain meaning."

I leaned forward in my armchair to get a better view of the street.

"Hullo."

"An observation of interest?"

"A brougham has just stopped at our front door. A fellow is stepping from the coach. He's approaching 221 and he's stepping smartly to get out of this beastly weather. The brougham is drawing away."

Holmes slouched into an attitude of indifference bordering on indolence.

"Good. I'll welcome any diversion from this fixation on Moriarty."

There came a knock at the door.

"A gentleman to see you, Mr. Holmes."

"Show him in, Mrs. Hudson."

Holmes' landlady duly showed in and left us alone with a rather dour fellow, dressed in modest tweeds. His age I estimated to be near thirty. Dreamy, melancholy eyes. A bushy moustache and sandy hair, worn on the long side but neatly combed across and back from a severe left part.

He looked from one of us to the other.

"Mr. Holmes?"

Holmes replied without rising. "I am he. This is my colleague and confidant, Doctor Watson, whom you may trust with all and any information that you entrust to me. And you are?"

"My name is Herbert Wells. I am associated with the Royal College of Science in South Kensington where I earn a meager personal income as a tutor." The melancholia in his hazel eyes deepened. "I should say straightaway that I'm not altogether certain that my problem, well, I'm not sure I will be able to pay you."

Coolness settled upon Holmes and seemed to chill the warmth of the sitting room.

"Indeed?"

"But I trust, sir, that the nature of the problem itself will enable me to draw and sustain your interest and efforts on my behalf."

"Mr. Wells, you may be right. Allow me to assess such likelihood by providing, please, a concise account of the circumstances that have brought you to me."

Our visitor took a seat, his back held straight, a prideful set to eyes and jaw.

"I am not only a tutor. I happen to be a published author."

I snapped my fingers.

"Of course. I should have recognized your name. Are you are H.G. Wells, by any chance?"

"I am."

"Well then," I said, "it's a distinct pleasure to

meet you, sir. I've read your work. *The Invisible Man* and *The War of the Worlds* are outstanding works of the imagination."

Wells' dour expression brightened. "Thank you, Doctor. Mr. Holmes, have you read my work?"

"Not the novels, I'm afraid. Watson's published narratives have quite sated my appetite for melo-dramas concocted to distract a semi-literate readership."

Wells burst to his feet.

"I happen to craft works of popular art for thinking readers! I did not come here to be insulted."

"I was about to add," said Holmes, "that I have read and found of interest your articles in *The Science School Journal* on the reformation of society. The notion of free love is an interesting concept. Your most provocative notion is that of a World State."

Wells remained standing, tweed cap bunched in his balled fists. But his anger and defiance of manner subsided.

"A World State is inevitable, gentlemen. Some mighty big eggs are going to get broken making that omelet, thus people back away. It will take more than one war, I fear, to ultimately lead us to the collective planetary consciousness necessary to undertake such an endeavor."

Holmes nodded. "A planned society, an end to nationalism, allowing people to progress by merit rather than birth. Yes, I am aware of your publication and your ideas. Would you, therefore, be so kind as to oblige me, Mr. Wells, by resuming your seat and letting me know how I may be of service?"

Wells harrumphed a muted chuckle.

"Forgive me. I was captain of the debating team, you see. It is my nature to take up the gauntlet when there is a difference of opinion."

"Understood. Pray proceed."

"I should begin then, I suppose, by saying that my latest novel is to be called *The Time Machine*."

"By Jove," said I, "that does sound intriguing."

Holmes admonished me with a glance and a terse, "Watson, please."

I settled back in my chair, determined to listen without further interruption.

Wells said, "The plot of the novel deals with a time traveler and like many of my novels embodies, as themes, those ideas expressed in my articles in the *Journal*, and theories resulting from my fascination with the whole notion of time travel. In fact, I am chairman of the United Kingdom's chapter of an international organization of scientists and enthusiasts like myself who share an interest in such a radical theory. We privately publish a quarterly journal to exchange and debate our ideas on the subject." His voice lowered to a conspiratorial whisper. "I will tell you in all confidentiality, Mr. Holmes, Doctor Watson, that I am in the process of constructing what I believe will be a time machine."

I could not contain my gasp of astonishment.

"Time travel? Is such a thing possible?"

Wells offered a wry smile. "In fiction, quite effectively. In reality... we shall see."

Holmes got a fresh bowl of tobacco going.

"I daresay, Mr. Wells, you have succeeded in piquing my curiosity. I expect some sinister party is out to take possession and/or otherwise exploit your invention."

The opportunity to differ with Holmes put a glint in Wells' eye.

"No, it's not that at all. My invention is secreted away, and I believe it cannot be found. She is safe enough. I've come to you because of a young man, a lad really, who has come to temporarily lodge with my wife and me. An extremely precocious teenager."

"A difficult age."

"First, though," said Wells, "some background on my home life."

"If it's pertinent."

"But that's just it, don't you see? I don't know what's pertinent and what isn't because, well, frankly, Mr. Holmes, I don't know what the blazes is going on! My wife and I have been married for only a few months, and I regret to say that there was considerable discord under our roof before our young lodger arrived." Wells cleared his throat. His eyes dropped to his shoes. "I seem to be one of those unfortunate souls cursed by uncontrollable romantic impulse."

Holmes said through a cloud of pipe smoke, "Ah. Free love."

"I married a cousin. We wed much too young. Then I fell in love with the girl who is now my wife. I was her tutor. That element of my history is the source of our discord."

"As a tutor, you remain in regular contact with other attractive young women and girls."

Wells sighed. "And, blast me for a fool, I too often yielded to temptation."

"You were saying about your house guest."

"Quite so. We corresponded voluminously after becoming acquainted through the organization, exchanging ideas on the subject of time travel both in our quarterly publication and in personal correspondence. I regarded his enthusiasm for my theories as, well... inordinate though frankly rather flattering. That said, my wife and I were shocked when the young man appeared—uninvited, mind you!--on our front step, having managed to travel alone all the way here with the express purpose of wanting to collaborate on my time machine. Ridiculous, of course, and I told him so. Still, well, uh, we took him in."

Mrs. Wells added, "It was only the Christian thing to do, considering his age. We have a guest room."

"He's sixteen," said Wells, "but the boy is, how shall I put it, well, he's intellectually brilliant and yet otherworldly. Socially awkward. He's the reason we've come to you, Mr. Holmes. The young man has vanished from our home without a trace. My wife and I don't know what to think or do. I feel responsible in large part for his being in London. I want you to find him."

"The boy's name?"

"His name is Albert. Albert Einstein."

CHAPTER 6

We caught a train from Waterloo Station. Wells and his wife lived in Woking, a large town and civil parish located in the west of Surrey.

Along the way, Wells and I struck up a conversation regarding the current crop of popular writers, resulting in a spirited debate over the comparative merits of two recent titles by H. Rider Haggard.

For his part, Holmes sat with his back held straight, staring at his reflection in the rain-streaked window glass and the passing world beyond, speaking not a word throughout the journey. He had often enough voiced his contempt for fiction in general, always upon publication of one of my stories.

"One gets quite enough fiction in the daily news," is how he would phrase it.

Maybury Road was a quiet, residential neighborhood. The hansom cab that brought us from the train station drew up before Number 143, a pleasant enough narrow, two-story structure similar to those abutting its either side.

It wasn't raining in Woking, but the day was damp and dreary.

An attractive young woman greeted us at the door.

"Darling, welcome home. Gentlemen, please come in."

She was slender, several years her husband's junior, with sandy hair and comely features. She stepped aside to allow us entry. Easing past her, I caught the faintest scent of jasmine perfume.

I followed Holmes into a tastefully furnished sitting room that was warmed by a cheery fire in the hearth.

Wells and his wife embraced briefly on the doorstep. She murmured something into his ear. She then closed the front door and they joined us.

Wells said, "Mr. Holmes, Doctor Watson, this is my wife, Sarah, though the family has always called her Jane."

Jane's eyes lowered.

"Please, Herbert. These gentlemen don't need to know about me."

Almost in unison, Holmes and I said, "How do you do?"

We received a short, polite nod in return. Her eyes remained downcast.

Wells said, "Mr. Holmes has consented to help us in trying to locate Albert."

Jane, for that is how I have chosen to refer to her, raised eyes bright with gratitude.

"Oh, thank you, sir!"

Holmes said, "What can you tell me about Albert? Your impressions of him?"

"Why, I guess first I would say that Albert is a most polite and soft-spoken lad, well brought-up. Rather socially awkward, though. And that's just it, don't you see? He has tremendous mental gifts and great personal commitment, traveling all this way to meet my husband. But if one is not accustomed to having children about--"

"Obnoxious little buggers, children," said Wells. "Demanding so much. I find it difficult to concentrate when they're about. Granted, they can become interesting, Albert being a prime example. The boy's a prodigy."

Jane said, "But he's a *boy*. I am accustomed to living alone with my husband, or to being left alone to myself."

"Do you have any idea where he could have gone, or why?"

"I do not." The terseness of her tone conveyed a nuance of emotion. "We rarely spoke, Alert and I. At our table, abstract enthusiasms, of which I freely admit to being completely oblivious, dominated dinnertime conversation."

The postman chose that moment to drop

envelopes through a mail slot adjacent to the front door, manuscript-sized envelopes among them. They scattered across the floor beneath the mail drop.

"Ah," said Wells.

He disengaged his arm from that of his wife and stooped to retrieve the mail.

Holmes said, "I should like to examine the guest's room."

"Certainly." Wells straightened and started down a short corridor that led to the rear of the house, absently scanning the letters and envelopes. "I'll show you."

I could have gone with them, but I decided that there was nothing my friend would miss. Holmes wanted me to stay behind and engage the lady of the house in dialogue, the purpose being to determine if she might know more about this matter than she had thus far let on.

A brief, awkward silence fell between us.

Two strangers left alone in each other's presence.

Her jasmine perfume, subtle yet more noticeable here inside the house, titillated my nostrils.

I admired Wells for having a spouse who wore perfume for her husband in the privacy of their home... though that was hardly a proper opening conversational gambit!

I said, "I regret this intrusion, Mrs. Wells. I'm sure my friend won't be long."

"Not at all, Doctor... Watson, was it?"

"Dr. John H. Watson, at your service."

"My husband, as you've no doubt observed, is a brilliant man."

"He's done quite well as an author."

"Indeed. Herbert is a fine writer, but upon reading his books you'll notice, I daresay, little regard for the feminine perspective, which I sense, Doctor, that you possess in abundance. Are you a practicing medical physician?"

"I am retired from private practice."

"Well, there you go." She placed a slim, manicured hand on my forearm. She smiled. "It is your bedside manner, wouldn't you say?"

"I'm, er, uh, sure that must be the case."

I felt a sudden warmth course through me, emanating from her touch. Quite frankly, I was tongue-tied.

She eased a bit closer to me without removing her fingertips from my sleeve.

"You will understand, Doctor, how rare it is for a woman to encounter a man who understands a woman."

At the sound of her husband and Holmes returning down the corridor, her hand dropped away. She stepped back to resume standing exactly where she had been.

I asked, "Any luck, Holmes?"

"No, but that's hardly surprising. Tell me, Mr. and Mrs. Wells, to the best of your knowledge, did young Albert socialize with anyone in London other than with you?"

Wells said, "Not that I know of."

"He had no friends that I knew of," said Jane.

"A young man, far from home and alone in a big city. Yes, he would stay to himself, if shy by nature."

Jane said, "He spent most of his time commandeering the kitchen table with his books and papers and pencils, scribbling out equations as if I wasn't there in my own kitchen."

Wells said, "Darling, aren't you being rather harsh in the boy's absence?"

"I'm sorry. I don't mean to be. He's not a pest, but he always is underfoot, it seems. Yet I fear for his safety, alone out there in the city." She said to Holmes, "He assured us that his family knew he was here and though they did not approve, they have come to accept his independent nature and ways. I did not feel that we were in any way harboring a mere runaway."

Wells nodded. "I spent a day showing him around the city. The Natural History Museum. A walk along the Thames."

Jane turned icy eyes on him. "And a visit to the music hall."

Wells sighed like a man severely and routinely put upon.

"My dear, Albert might as well observe lowbrow culture as well as highbrow."

Holmes said, "And why should that be, if I may ask?"

Jane continued to glare at her husband. "You may

well ask that, Mr. Holmes. I'd like to know the answer myself. They went to The Empire in the West End, the most notorious of those so-called 'pleasure palaces.'"

"My dear," said Wells, "we've dined there ourselves."

"At your insistence. The comedians were vulgar. The ballet dancers, well, they were far more Eros than Bolshoi, and certainly nothing a naive young man need be exposed to unless you intend to introduce him to vices of your own. Do you go to The Empire often, Herbert?"

Silence descended.

Holmes said, "Come, Watson. We're finished here." A curt nod. "Mrs. Wells, a thousand pardons for this invasion of your privacy."

She blinked, momentarily taken aback.

"That's kind of you to say, Mr. Holmes. We only want Albert found. It's been a pleasure meeting you. And you, Doctor Watson."

This last was accompanied by a direct gaze that warmed me as had her touch, right there in front of her husband in their cozy living room!

"My pleasure, Mrs. Wells."

"Please, call me Jane."

Wells said, "I'll show you gentlemen out."

A drizzling mist had begun while we were indoors. Holmes and I turned up the collars of our coats in preparation for crossing to the Hansom that Holmes had retained to wait for us.

He said, "I shall be in touch. You will hear from me directly when we have located this wandering lad."

"But how will you undertake such a task? London is so great a city. Where will you start?"

"My dear sir," said Holmes, "you have retained me to locate the boy. This I intend to do. But you will kindly respect the fact that my methods are my own. I hold myself accountable to no one until satisfactory results are achieved. That is acceptable to you?"

"Certainly. I meant no offense." Wells gestured with the manuscript envelopes that had come in the mail, which he still held in his left hand. "I have much work to occupy my attention. My publisher, damn him, wants revisions on a novel in progress! Also, there is, er, the, uh, 'other project' that I'm constructing and have almost completed. I have much to keep me busy. I will expect to hear from you, Mr. Holmes, when you have located Albert. Good day, gentlemen."

CHAPTER 7

Holmes said, "What do you make of it, Watson?"

Our horse's hooves clattered away from Maybury Road.

I said, "It seems that Wells has his share of domestic difficulty."

"The wife's display of jealousy, you mean, about his attending the music hall? Jealousy is the province of woman."

"I'm not referring to that. Holmes, I'm damned if Mrs. Wells didn't shamelessly flirt with me after you and her husband left us alone."

Holmes' keen eyes glinted with barely muted interest and amusement.

"And did you resist?"

"I barely had the chance! But it was overt, I'll tell you that. There was closeness, touch, and those eyes of hers! It was quite improper."

"But not intolerable?"

"Well uh, you and Wells returned. I barely had the opportunity to say anything."

"You have no doubt considered that her behavior in all likelihood had nothing to do with your manly charms."

"A diversionary tactic intended to keep me from asking questions?"

"It would seem likely."

"Holmes, what do you know that I don't know?"

He reached into an inner coat pocket and withdrew a lady's dainty kerchief, which he handed to me.

I noted the embroidered initials.

"*S.W.*," I read aloud. "Sarah Wells. Where did you find it?"

"Under a stack of male undergarments in a dresser in Albert Einstein's room."

"Did her husband see you find it?"

"He thinks that he saw what I was doing, but he did not *observe* what I was doing. He was too busy standing in the hallway, glancing over the return addresses on those envelopes that came in the mail."

I returned the kerchief to Holmes. Jane's jasmine perfume, emanating from it, again tantalized my nostrils.

"Do you think the boy stole it from her belongings?"

"That is one possibility. Or it could have been a personal, one could say intimate, gift from the lady of the house to their young houseguest."

"You suspect Mrs. Wells and this Albert of having a romantic dalliance?"

"Tactfully phrased, Watson, as ever. It is a possibility, is it not?"

"After her behavior toward me, I suppose so."

"Tell me, Watson, since you were so favorably impressed by Mr. Wells. How do you think he would react to learning that his wife was guilty of such infidelity?"

I tugged an earlobe. "He is an English gentleman, an intense fellow as all artists are, and a proud man."

"A man of direct action, would you say?"

"He gives that impression. Are you suggesting that H.G. Wells somehow did away with the boy when he found out that something was going on between his wife and Albert? If that's the case, then his whole effort to engage you to locate the boy is just a ruse to throw off suspicion."

"We need more facts," said Holmes. "I should like to know more about Wells' time machine. But for now, or perhaps as a step in that direction..." He again dipped a hand into a coat pocket, this time producing a piece of paper that had been neatly folded. He handed it to me. "I found this in a jacket in Albert's closet after I'd filched the kerchief from the dresser drawer. Incidentally, I also managed a glance at the return addresses as Wells shuffled through his envelopes."

He named three well-known popular weekly magazines.

I said, as I unfolded the sheet of paper, "I'm not only familiar with those magazines; two of them have published my stories."

The piece of paper was a cheaply produced flyer:

The Empire Music Hall
Leicester Square
New Shows Weekly! Matinees Daily!

Beneath this was an oval picture of a lovely young woman with a wild mane of untamed raven black curls that spilled across bare shoulders. She had a wide smile and an extremely low-cut dress.

To Albert was written in feminine script across the picture, and was signed, *Danielle*.

Holmes said, "Albert, it seems, may be carrying on a dalliance of his own, at the pleasure palace Mrs. Wells so despises."

"I assume then that our next stop then is to be The Empire Theater."

"An interview with Danielle could well yield useful information."

I studied the lovely girl in the picture.

"There are worse ways to spend a rainy afternoon, I daresay."

He lapsed into a thoughtful silence as our Hansom cab approached the railway station.

Edginess coursed through me, drawing taut my nerves with impatience. My encounter with Mrs. Wells had left an unpleasant aftertaste in my mouth, not to mention the possibility, even the likelihood, of her dalliance with the boy we intended to find.

What a tangled web of human emotions!

A futurist author.

His restless, promiscuous wife.

And a young lad who spent his time poring over mathematical equations while finding time for Lord knows what else in the area of romantic liaisons.

So many unanswered questions.

What had become of Moriarty? He was still at large. What ungodly scheme was that twisted, brilliant mind up to?

Zombies!

It was unthinkable that such an evil could stalk the civilized world, and worse still that a man of Professor Moriarty's insane genius could somehow summon them to carry out his nefarious bidding.

I had no doubt that we would again encounter the Professor.

But for now, there existed only one immediate objective, and nothing would be gained by heeding distractions.

Where was Albert Einstein?

CHAPTER 8

Waterloo Station throbbed with the clatter and racket of arriving and departing trains and the chatter of human conversation and movement. The piercing shouts of a newsboy spouting the latest headlines cut through the din.

The newsboy was a scruffy lad of fourteen. A smattering of freckles dusted his pug nose. The corner of his mouth curled up in a natural sneer. A steady stream of people slowed only slightly to place coins into his right palm. These coins were dropped into a leather pouch worn at his waist while the boy handed over the newspapers in a continuous, smoothly repetitive motion.

Holmes waited until there was a break in the line of customers.

"I say, Wiggins, a minute of your time, if you please."

The boy's natural sneer became a toothy grin.

"Mr. Holmes! It's been a while. How've you been, guv'nor?"

"I endure life with my usual degree of interest, if not enthusiasm. And you, Wiggins? How are my Baker Street Irregulars?"

Wiggins was a homeless orphan of the streets. That is all I knew about him. He was one of a network of such street urchins that Holmes had organized, funded and often utilized. No one paid attention to children like Wiggins who came and went seemingly everywhere in the city while in the process managing to hear everything that constituted the gossip of virtually every social class. The original Baker Street Irregulars had been small in number and, as the name suggested, had initially been based out of the immediate vicinity of Holmes' flat. But over the years their number had grown to the point that the Irregulars had come to serve as Holmes' finger on the human pulse of the city, able to go everywhere, see everything and overhear everyone.

Wiggins practically assumed a position of attention.

"We're just fine, guv'nor. Me? A fella never has to work if he enjoys his labors and I enjoy selling papers to the toffs right here in Waterloo Station. Now, how may I be of service?"

"For starters, while you're standing here doing what you so love to do, you can keep a lookout for a passenger disembarking from a train from Surrey."

"I'm your man, guv'nor! I can do that right enough."

"I have two tasks for you. You will, therefore, need to delegate authority."

"Done it before, Mr. Holmes, I can do it again."

A glance at the boy's normally reddened knuckles and the scar tissue over one eye bespoke a fondness for brawling. Wiggins did not always get along well with others, even with his fellow Baker Street Irregulars.

Holmes said, "I trust, Wiggins, that you will keep your baser instincts in check."

"Aw, sir, I don't mean no harm. Sometimes one of the other fellas just gets on me nerves and, well, I just sort of snap, you could say."

"I say that this time, you will put the mission first."

Wiggins looked contrite.

"I hear and obey, Mr. Holmes."

The boy's unusual choice of words, "*I hear and obey*," was a catchphrase popular of late in everyday conversation, its source a line from the novel *She*, by H. Rider Haggard, the author whom Wells and I had been discussing earlier. The popular fiction Holmes so despised was exactly that... popular. I noted copies of Haggard's latest novel in a bookstall nearby, the Haggard book flanked by several other popular titles, including *War of the Worlds* by H.G. Wells.

"With the arriving trains from Surrey under

surveillance," said Holmes, "the next step is to locate a young man who is somewhere in the city. Sixteen years of age. Has been described as socially awkward. His name is Albert Einstein, and he is presently perhaps wandering idly and seeing the sights, or is perhaps in dalliance with a lady friend, or perhaps has been or is about to be a victim of foul play."

"Uh, that's not much to go on, guv'nor."

"Believe me, Wiggins, in that I share in your disappointment. Albert is a visitor to our city. He's a German national but speaks English. A gifted mathematician. This needs to be given top priority."

"A tall order, Mr. Holmes, but if anyone can find that needle a haystack, I reckon it's the Baker Street Irregulars."

"I reckon it is," said Holmes.

Ignoring the passers-by who wanted to buy his newspapers, Wiggins indicated a scruffy, thin child of eight or so, who was engaged in polishing a gentlemen's boots.

"That's Timmy. He don't look like much but he flies like an eagle. He'll see to it that word of missing Albert gets spread and fast. And you say this other gent is coming in from Surrey?"

"He may, he may not," said Holmes, "but if he comes to London, I want to know about it." He proceeded to render a concise and specific description of H.G. Wells from age to height to appearance to a certain gait in Wells' walk that I too had noticed.

Wiggins listened attentively.

"Is he dangerous, guv'nor? Not that it would matter none to me, of course, but some of the other fellers would be better off knowing in advance."

"No, he's not dangerous in the way you mean," said Holmes. "He's a teacher. A writer. The only danger he poses is abstract."

"Abstract, guv'nor?"

"His mind, Wiggins. The mind is the most dangerous weapon. Always remember that."

"I don't know about that, Mr. Holmes. A black-jack, well applied, can make scrambled eggs out of anyone's mind."

Holmes chuckled. "Quite so, Wiggins. Quite so. You are a man of admirably direct temperament. If the gentleman, a Mr. Wells by name, does show himself, I want him followed."

"We'll be on it, sir, me and Timmy. If I spy the gent, we'll stick to him. One of us ahead, the other behind. He won't give us the slip, and he won't know he's being tailed. Count on us."

"I do, Wiggins. Pity I don't have a picture for you."

I cleared my throat. I crossed to the bookseller.

While I made my purchase, Holmes and the newsboy summoned Timmy, with whom they conferred.

When I rejoined them, I handed Holmes a copy of *War of the Worlds*, the dust jacket's back flap open to expose a recent photograph of the author.

"Thank you, Watson. So glad you deigned, at last,

to return from observer to participant status." He handed the book with the photo of Wells to Wiggins, who shared the picture with Timmy. "That's it then. Wiggins, get the word out on Mr. Einstein, and stay vigilant should Mr. Wells put in an appearance. I will expect regular updates."

CHAPTER 9

The Empire Theater was doing a grand business for a weekday afternoon, or perhaps precisely *because* it was a gloomy, rainy workday.

We paused just inside the main entrance.

Nearly three hundred people crowded the noisy, spacious main room that sported twin bars that faced one another along opposite walls running the length of the establishment. Tables and booths over-flowed with boisterous patrons who ate, drank, and made merry. The atmosphere was rank, noisy, and hazy with smoke.

Everywhere there was something to see. High overhead, a lovely woman on a trapeze glided with joy and grace. There were the *tableau vivants*: small, well-lighted sets where female performers posed as "real life" pictures.

I had trouble taking my eyes from the one nearest

us, which a placard identified as *Diane the Huntress*. A proud Amazonian blonde, with a stuffed but quite realistic-appearing lion crouched at her feet, stood as if caught in the act of turning away, her left breast and derriere in profile. A perfectly proportioned, shapely, muscular body and she appeared to be nude although I had read that these models actually wore flesh-colored body stockings. Further along was another *tableau vivant* entitled *Nymphs Bathing*.

A family of acrobats was concluding their performance onstage to drunken hooting and heckling amid sparse applause. The acrobats bowed and nimbly pranced off-stage, to be replaced by a pair of comedians. It was impossible to hear their jokes this far back.

I said, "It is all quite enough to make an impression on a young man visiting London."

Holmes said, "There's a table."

He brought an elbow into play. We made our way through to a table midway back from the stage and off to the side, from which an inebriated fellow in laborer's clothes and his equally inebriated doxy shambled past us on their way out.

A portly waiter with a handlebar moustache and a stained apron appeared almost instantly to clear the table.

"What can I get for you, gentlemen?"

Holmes' hands steepled so that the fingertips touched his chin. He stared straight ahead, not at the stage.

"You can fetch us Danielle. We would speak with her on a matter of importance."

"Uh sorry, gents, but the performers ain't allowed to mingle."

"Tell her we're not the police. Tell her that if she tries to run, we will find her. Sparing us a few minutes of her time now will be a minimal inconvenience compared to trying to dodge us."

"Yes, sir. And the name, sir?"

Holmes told him. The waiter withdrew. Holmes assumed an air of patient stoicism.

Inwardly, I chastised myself for not coming armed, but when we'd left Baker Street that day, it had been for no more than a train ride to the Wells home in Surrey.

The Empire's clientele had come to have a good time, but a significant percentage of those present, men and women, would not think twice about slipping a stiletto between a man's ribs from behind for the price of cab fare home.

I said, "Do you think that was wise, bandying your name about in, well, a place like this?"

"I thought it best. The social stratum we're presently dealing with here may not recognize me on sight, but they will know my name."

"Precisely my point. So, we're to expect a less than cordial reception?"

"The sooner the better then," said he. "We came here for results, did we not?"

A towering figure materialized from the crowd

behind Holmes, roughly shoving people aside. The fellow was broad-shouldered and over six feet tall.

I said, "Here comes result number one."

The man's ham-sized hand rested on my friend's shoulder.

"Well, if it ain't Mr. Sherlock Holmes, come calling where he don't belong."

Holmes half-rose, half-turned. One arm snaked around the man's thick arm. The other captured the big fellow in a headlock. Holmes twisted sharply, using the man's own strength against him. He flipped the man over his shoulder.

I leapt to my feet, stepping away just in time to avoid the big fellow landing on his back full force upon the wooden table, crushing our table into kindling beneath the impact of his weight.

A brief hush. Then booming, earthy laughter. Conversation and merrymaking resumed at the surrounding tables.

The booming laughter continued. The giant picked himself off the floor. He was the source of the laughter.

I didn't know what to expect. Did he have friends about to rush us? I drew up my fists, ready for a fight. Then I lowered my fists.

Holmes was smiling. Not that quirk-of-the-lips hint of a smile that I was used to, but a full-on almost boyish grin of recognition.

"Hello, Nappy. I thought you knew that I granted no man the right to lay a hand on me."

Up close, the bruiser appeared even bigger and wider. A giant of a man, craggy of face and wild of eye. Nappy red hair, worn short, clung to his head like a strange cap. His ugly face shone with a wide grin.

"I did not know that, Mr. Holmes, but I certainly knows it now! You never come visit me once after they sent up."

"I'm a busy man, Nappy. Too busy to stay in touch with every crook I put away. But you're a free man again. I see you've not changed your taste for the gaudier side of life."

"If you mean betting on the nags and chasing the skirts, right you are, Mr. Holmes, and The Empire is the ideal place for both! Track touts with inside tips a fella can use and, well, you can see for yourself by looking about that the pickings is ripe for any bloke what got him an itch to chase women, cause it don't take much chasin'. But don't you worry none about me, Mr. Holmes. Me crook days is behind me. It's honest work what keeps me busy here. They call me a bouncer." He chuckled and brushed away a spec of remaining dust from a broad shoulder. "Though I reckon t'was me got bounced by you this time."

"Nappy, I'm rather glad to see you too."

The big man offered his hand. "When that waiter told me who it was poking around, I had to come over and say hullo. Reckon I came on a bit over-friendly."

They shared a hearty handshake.

"Nappy, I want you to meet my good friend, Doctor Watson. John H. Watson, this is Nappy McGuire. I sent Nappy up for two-to-five, wasn't it, Nappy?"

The ugly giant again proffered his ham-like hand, and so we shook hands. His grip was firm to the point of grinding my knuckles.

"A counterfeit rap, it was. Dr. Watson, your friend here is the finest gent in all of London and, believe me, Nappy McGuire is a boy what's been around. Know what he done?"

I retrieved my hand from his grip. The knuckles ached but nothing seemed to be broken.

"Uh, no..."

"When he sicced the coppers on me, it was for a one-time job I done to pay for me mother to have an operation."

I said, with what I hoped was a touch of levity, "My dear fellow, you needn't offer your defense to me. I'm not the prosecutor."

He glowered.

"You calling me a liar?"

Holmes reached up and placed a restraining hand on a massive shoulder.

"He meant no offense, Nappy. We're here on business. We can use your help."

"Well, all right," Nappy said. "Any friend of yours, Mr. Holmes." He turned to me with that huge grin plastered across his broad face. "After I was sent up, Mr. Holmes claimed the reward."

I said, "Pardon me for saying so, Nappy, but you seem remarkably forgiving of the man who put you behind bars. And you, Holmes. It's extremely unusual for you to accept a reward."

"This," said Holmes, "was an exception."

"Yuh see," said Nappy, "after Mr. Holmes cashed the reward, know what he done with it? He handed over every last shilling to pay for me mother's operation. It saved her life."

Holmes said, "And how is the old dear?"

Nappy guffawed. "Oh, Mum's fit and ornery as the day she had me." Then his craggy features grew serious.

"And Danielle? She does perform here?"

"Aye. Dani's about to go on, soon as these jokers are off."

The curtain closed on the comedians, who were taking their bows to another smattering of applause intermingled with catcalls and heckling.

Holmes said, "We'll require only a minute of her time. By the way, Nappy, you don't happen to recall a German teenager named Albert as numbering among Danielle's recent admirers?"

Nappy rubbed his lantern jaw.

"Dani's the one to talk to."

"I would impose upon you to introduce us."

"Glad to! A tasty little morsel she is, though no one knows much about her. She came with Andre as part of his act?"

"Andre?"

"The knife thrower. This way. They're about to go on. We'd best hurry."

CHAPTER 10

We followed Nappy down the broad main aisle to the front of the music hall. At the orchestra pit, we cut across, passed the front rows. A door led backstage.

And there, in the wings of the stage, stood Danielle.

There are many types of feminine beauty. Holmes often chides me for being a romantic at heart, as if that were a weakness. There's the beauty of my Mary: clear-eyed, steadfast, peaches-and-cream complexioned. There is the languid, smoldering beauty of Jane Wells, sensuality incarnate.

And there is the beauty of one like Danielle.

No more than nineteen years old. She belonged on the stage, where radiant beauty like hers could be appreciated; an essence of beauty mostly physical yet which exuded a somehow wholesome quality that touched the schoolboy that always lives deep within most men. A woman-child. Untamed hair that shone in the stage lights. A sparkle in her eyes and smiling. Her stage costume revealed lovely, long legs.

Stagehands scampered about, setting up a backboard support center stage.

In the wings on the opposite side of the stage, a dark young man, his features partly concealed by shadow, busied himself straightening rows of long-bladed knives that rested upon a wheeled table.

Andre.

Satisfied, he allowed the stagehands to wheel the table upstage from the backboard, upon which a chalk outline closely approximated Danielle's figure.

She turned her sparkling smile on us upon our approach. This young woman, who apparently intended within the next minute or so to stand against that board while knives were thrown at her, exuded the effervescence of a high society ingénue at her coming out party.

"Yes?"

Nappy said, "Dani, this is Mr. Sherlock Holmes."

She blinked. Her eyes widened.

"Mr. Sherlock Holmes, the detective?"

"One and the same," said Holmes.

She extended her hand in the Continental fashion. "A pleasure to meet you, I'm sure." Her tone and manner of speech were not in Nappy's coarse Cockney but carried the lilt of breeding and education.

Holmes leaned forward and kissed the back of her slim, tapered fingers in the Continental fashion.

"I do apologize for intruding here on your job, Miss—" He let the sentence taper off into a query.

Nappy said, "Y'know, now that he mentions it, Dani, I've never heard your last name bandied about."

From the wings opposite, Andre strode to center stage., revealing himself to be a lean fellow, his dark hair curled over his collar. He wore black. He looked pointedly in our direction.

Danielle said, "Mr. Holmes, I'm due on stage. What is it you want of me?"

"I'd like to ask you briefly about a young man. He's sixteen years old. German. He's attended your performance, perhaps more than once."

From the pit, the orchestra struck up a fanfare.

Dani cast a nervous glance at Andre.

"I'm sorry, I can't help you."

Holmes drew from his pocket the flyer bearing her signed photograph, allowing her to clearly see her signature.

"His name is Albert. Albert Einstein."

"I'm sorry, Mr. Holmes, but on a good day I sign fifty or a hundred of those flyers. I know nothing about your missing German boy."

From the stage, André said, "Danielle." Her name on his lips sounded cold as a knife blade.

Dani said, "Excuse me, gentlemen."

She flitted away on those lovely legs. She and her partner exchanged words. They spoke without looking in our direction. Andre's demeanor was intense.

Nappy said, "Uh, Mr. Holmes. I caught a gander of this lad you're asking about. Dani signed her picture for him yesterday, at the morning show it was. Before that, before she went on, I happened to be walking by his table when he ordered a cup of tea. Tea, mind you, in a place like this! He had a German accent, right enough."

"I asked you about him, Nappy. Why didn't you tell me straightaway? Do you have something to hide?"

Nappy snickered. "Who don't? But nothing to do with this, I assure you. I figured it was between you and Dani. That kraut boy was here again today for the morning show. Him and her talked some, they did. Then the German kid left. I figured she'd tell you about that. But she lied. Y'know one ting I've learned in my life's misadventures, Mr. Holmes? Women are funny."

"Nappy, your grasp of the obvious is matched only by your physical endurance."

"Huh?"

Onstage, the curtains parted. The orchestra began playing a low-keyed mood piece. The incessant chatter of the audience died down.

Andre and Danielle took a bow, whereupon Dani's shapely bare legs carried her in the direction of the backboard.

I said, "Holmes, she referred to the boy as missing. You never told her that we were looking for Albert because he's missing."

That got me the flicker of a smile.

"Very good, Watson."

Andre remained facing the audience, seeming to check the balance of the steel blade in his hand. This could only have been for the benefit of the audience. Andre surely well knew the tools of his trade. The mounting anticipation in the hall became a palpable thing that rippled across the stage to where the three of us—myself, Holmes and Nappy—stood grouped together in the wings.

Nappy said in a low voice, "There's something else, Mr. Holmes, though I don't reckon it's connected with whatever has brought you here. But the word is out on you."

I frowned. "The word?"

Holmes nodded, keen eyes thoughtful.

"So, the word has gone out to hunt me down."

"Aye, guv'nor. I heard tell of it not ten minute before you gents walked in. The underworld is on alert. You're a walking target. There's profit for the lad or gang what takes you down. I just heard a couple of blokes laying odds that you won't last twenty-four hours."

Holmes regarded me with a single arched eyebrow.

"What do you say, Watson? Dangerous men lurking around every corner, poised to attack when least expected with the intention of killing me. As you are often in my general vicinity of late, I should advise—"

"Trust me, Holmes, I consider this development a direct threat against my personal safety as well as to yours. Now I really wish I was packing hardware."

Nappy eased aside the lapel of his jacket. A heavy .44 revolver rode in a shoulder holster beneath his left arm.

"If anything happens in *my* vicinity, you can bloody well believe that this bouncer is primed and ready."

Onstage, Danielle pirouetted gracefully before placing her back to the board in a pose that naturally brought her hips and breasts into prominence. Andre hurled the first knife. It quivered into the board, its ornate handle quivering less than an inch from Danielle's left ear. This elicited a collective gasp from the crowd. Danielle, however, did not bat an eye.

I felt myself growing edgy again. No matter that this was a well-rehearsed routine performed many times before, I am not a man to comfortably stand by while knives are thrown.

Andre, grim of face and narrow of eye, threw his second knife... *straight at my companion!*

In the stage lights, the knife's blade glinted in furious flight.

I had only time to shout, "Holmes, *look out!*"

CHAPTER 11

A woman in the audience screamed.

There was no time for me to lunge at Holmes to heave my friend out of the knife's path. No time for Holmes to dodge injury even after I drew his attention to the impending danger.

Only Nappy found time to react in those fleeting seconds through the simple expedient of lifting his huge right hand, palm forward, in an automatic reflex. The knife pierced the hand as if Nappy had purposefully caught it, the knife's handle protruding from his palm while the blade, slick with dripping blood, extended from the back of his hand.

Nappy emitted a grunt. He faltered but remained standing, clasping the wrist tightly beneath the injured hand.

"Damn, that smarts!"

Holmes said, "Stout fellow, Nappy. You saved my life."

Nappy winced. "That's for saving me mum's life."

Everything happened at once after that. Andre whirled, sprinting for the opposite side of the stage. Danielle scampered after him.

I gripped Nappy's arm with both hands.

"That knife's got to come out fast."

"Aye, Doctor. Make quick work of it, gents. I'll not scream like a girl."

I steadied Nappy's arm. Holmes slid the blade from the hand. Strands of gory flesh tissue drooled from the blade. I grabbed a bar rag from a nearby table and wrapped it around Nappy's wrist as an emergency tourniquet.

I flung open a lapel of Nappy's coat, revealing the .44 in its shoulder holster.

"May I?"

"With my blessing. Take it and get them snakes in the grass!" He continued applying pressure to the veins at his wrist. The trickle of blood had subsided.

I relieved him of the gun.

"See to it that your wound is properly dressed."

"Forget about me. They're getting away!"

He was right. Holmes had given chase. I left Nappy and joined him, racing across the stage in pursuit of Andre and Danielle.

Disconcerted rabble of the audience washed over us. The orchestra started playing a peppy number while a tuxedoed master of ceremonies made placating gestures with both hands, assuring the crowd that what they were witnessing was all part of the show, folks!

As he passed Andre's wheeled table, Holmes snared one of the knives. We reached a heavy metal backstage door that was still in the process of swinging shut. I took point, since I had the pistol, shouldering open the door with Holmes at my heels.

A shrouding mist beneath the black midday sky dappled rain puddles that spotted the alley like scattered discs of silver. Footfalls hurried away from us in either direction. Like any self-respecting criminals attempting to elude pursuit, they had separated, Danielle halfway to the mouth of the alley where it fed onto busy Leicester Square while André was taking off in the opposite direction.

Since I was closest to Danielle, I charged her after her.

She was clearly in my sight, having almost reached the cross-flow of pedestrian and vehicular traffic at that end of the alley. People with umbrellas, their outer garments wrapped tightly about them, scurried to whatever imperative destination had forced them into these inclement conditions. There was the brittle clacking of passing hooves and carriage wheels on wet pavement.

Then I lost sight of her amid a cluster of peddlers. I clearly heard the *click-clack-click* of her high-heeled boots. Then a quick glimpse of that saucy backside darting around a corner.

The peddlers left in her wake leaned forward,

their jaws agape from the vision of a gorgeous young woman, clad only in sparse, sparkly stage attire, flashing like a fantasy through their midst.

No more than thirty seconds behind her, I eased Nappy's pistol under my coat so it would not be visible and cause complications. I barreled through the clot of peddlers, overhearing remarks indicating a collective lingering doubt. *Was she real? An illusion, perhaps. An angel appearing among us! Naw, wise up. 'Twas only that chippie from The Empire. Aye, but an angel just the same.* Then I was through their ranks, reaching where the alley gave onto the Square.

A tumult was erupting in Leicester Square. Beyond my immediate line of vision, people started shouting in panic and surprise. Horses whinnied in panic. A runaway drawing and carriage bolted past, the animal's eyes wild with fear.

What the devil?!

Then I saw it. *Too late!*

One of those steam-powered, futuristic motor carriages identical to the ones I recalled from Castle Moriarty! The over-sized vehicle was speeding away, withdrawing at an alarming rate, a trail of steam and fiery sparks nosily spewing in its wake.

I lifted the revolver, started to take aim but held my fire. Everywhere around me, people were craning their necks to gawk, bystanders gathering down-range for a better view of the incredible machine roaring away.

I lowered the .44.

Someone in that strange contraption had either been waiting for Danielle or had somehow otherwise managed to appear on the scene to whisk her away.

A pistol shot cracked from the alley behind me.

I ran toward the gunfire. Around me, disoriented onlookers were scattering like startled pigeons.

In the alley, I found Holmes crouched for cover behind a pyramid of stacked crates. Andre held a pistol that he must have worn concealed. Andre's attention was on firing at Holmes. He had not yet seen me. He fired again.

The sound of a ricochet.

I raised and bent my left elbow, resting the barrel of the .44 on the elbow to steady my aim. This would be quick work, plunking one right through Andre's brainpan. I eased into the trigger pull.

Holmes saw me.

"No, Watson! We want him alive for interrogation!"

I eased up on the trigger pull.

Holmes left the cover of the crates in a somersault, righting himself onto one knee. He flung his knife before a startled Andre could fire.

The blade took Andre high in the right shoulder. He didn't make a sound when the impact jarred him sideways. Then he surprised me and perhaps Holmes as well. He did not continue his run for the far end of the alley. Instead, he leapt up, caught hold of the lowest rung of a fire escape with his good arm. Using the strength of both legs to compensate for having the use of only one arm, he commenced scrambling up the fire escape like a monkey climbing a coconut tree.

We continued the pursuit.

By the time I gained the fire escape, Holmes was already well overhead, stepping onto the rooftop. I hurried up after him. The metal rungs of the fire escape were slippery from the rain, but I made good progress without losing hold of the pistol. I reached the flat roof.

Andre was cornered near a small structure that provided rooftop access from inside the building. The structure was topped by a flagpole without a flag this rainy day. Andre had lost his gun along the way. He had tugged Homes' knife from his shoulder, using it to hold Holmes at bay with wide defensive swipes.

Holmes said to me, "Danielle?"

"The little minx had help waiting. One of Moriarty's super motor carriages."

Holmes indicated Andre.

"I'm not quite certain what this fellow has in mind. His surest way out would have been to run away and lose himself in the crowd."

Andre laughed. The laugh was not quite sane. Another swiping gesture with the knife.

"You will not take me. I have the protection of a powerful force!"

I said, "We can take him together. It's only a knife wielded by a wounded man."

Andre staggered. Another swipe with the bloodied blade.

"Try! I dare you."

Holmes said, "On the count of three."

But he did not even make the one-count, or if he did, I didn't hear it.

Every sound, every sensation, was abruptly drowned out at that moment by a bizarre, pervasive, thundering *whompa!-whompa!-whompa!* that vibrated the atmosphere with its throbbing, rhythmic palpitations, growing louder and louder.

CHAPTER 12

A flying machine of sleek black metal zoomed in from the low clouds like some bloated, evil insect.

The source of the *whompa!-whompa!-whompa!* that hammered the air came from the mighty steam engine that powered twin blades atop the aircraft. The propellers beat the thick damp air at an astonishing rate, creating the optical illusion of a large saucer hovering over us.

A pilot sat at the controls behind a wide windscreen that curved around the front. An ungainly human-like hulk stood at an open side door behind some sort of futuristic mounted weapon defined by a long muzzle that protruded from the craft.

The muzzle swiveled in Holmes' direction.

A rattling crackle. A bluish-white bolt like lightning lanced out from the muzzle. A small explosion and a cloud of smoke where Holmes had been seconds earlier before flinging himself behind the small structure at the foot of the flagpole.

Andre laughed his insane laugh. He raised both hands.

"Take me away!" He screamed as if this was the Second Coming. "*Take me, I say!*"

The muzzle shifted in his direction. I couldn't get a good enough look at whoever manned the weapon except to see that the body was abnormally proportioned. The muzzle unleashed another lancing bolt of bluish white light accompanied by loud crackling and popping.

The lightning bolt struck Andre. His body convulsed. He performed a crazed and savage dance. Then he exploded. There is no other word for it. One moment the man shimmied and shuddered as if possessed by a demon. Then the white light, a puff of smoke and Andre the knife thrower ceased to exist. Evaporated. Disappeared... except for a slight mound of gray ash on the spot where he'd stood.

I could scarcely believe my eyes! I forced myself to stop staring.

I brought up the .44 into target acquisition and took aim at the oversized figure that I could now see leaping about with odd, jerky movements behind the muzzle of the strange weapon. I triggered off one-two-three rounds in rapid succession.

The impact of my heavy bullets knocked the big figure backward into the cabin of the flying machine with such force that he rebounded from striking something inside and stumbled forward, toppling uncontrollably through the open side door.

I leapt back an instant before he landed with a *thud!* that made the rooftop shudder under my feet.

The gyro craft started to bank away.

Holmes was working fiercely at unscrewing the flagpole from its base, leaning into the task with maximum effort.

The fallen, broken body that had landed near me... *began to move!*

Slowly, steadily, with those strange twitching, jerking tremors, it first regained a knee and then rose to its feet. *It* is precisely the word. It moved with an abnormal, obscene sort of animation. The bullet holes I'd placed in its chest were plain enough, and the exit wound of each would be the size of a cricket ball. A quarter of his head was missing; the left side, from just above the eye to past the hairline. But his eyes were hungry!

A zombie!

It started for me, arms outstretched, hands grasping, the sickening dead stench reaching out for me as surely as those rotting fingers. The icy fingers found my throat. The thing closed in, its fetid mouth open wide, going for my neck.

I gave it the muzzle of the .44 instead. I rammed the gun barrel into its mouth. I pulled the trigger twice.

Its head erupted into a hideous, powdery cloud. It stumbled about, both hands frantically feeling the ruin where its head had been. Then it fell onto its knees. Then onto its face. The headless horror did not move.

Holmes succeeded in prying loose the flagpole from its base. He hurled the flagpole like a javelin. It flew unerringly, lodging itself between the churning propeller blades of the flying machine.

Abrupt silence when the propellers stopped. A startled cry from inside the aircraft. Then it plummeted to the pavement below, directly in front of The Empire Theater, and burst into a noisy orange-red fireball.

We surveyed the scene from the rooftop.

The flames that rose from the machine's unrecognizable remains were becoming encircled by onlookers.

"Nice throw."

He nodded. "Quite a day for Leicester Square. A murder attempt in the music hall, upstaged by an incredible flying machine that dramatically crashes and burns, leaving behind a headless zombie. I daresay the mundane song and dance routines will have a difficult time topping that."

The clang of approaching official wagons carried to us from several blocks away, closing fast. I scanned the rooftop. The zombie's headless form remained unmoving. Andre's ashes had been muddied by the unrelenting mist.

I said, "Time to initiate a tactful withdrawal.

Here I am back to blowing away zombies when I should be at home relaxing with my wife."

Holmes said, "The appearance of Moriarty's machines is hardly insignificant. It links him with the elusive Danielle, which in turn links Moriarty to the missing boy who is so enthralled with Danielle."

"But why would a world-class criminal like Moriarty waste his time with--" Then it came to me. "Ah. If Moriarty is aware of the boy's connection to H.G. Wells, is he also aware of the time machine Wells claims to have built?"

"Not a pretty picture, is it?" said Holmes. "An evil genius. A time machine. Zombies. An ugly mix. A complex web. We need more information."

A sigh worked its way up from my boot heels.

"I need a straight up whiskey."

"Capital idea, Watson." He indicated the fire escape. "Please lead the way."

CHAPTER 13

Wiggins was waiting for us on the front stoop of 221B
Baker Street. He leapt to his feet at first sight of
Holmes, his fourteen-year-old freckled face beaming
with enthusiasm. He threw a thumb over his
shoulder in the direction of the front door.

"That Mrs. Hudson, she don't even want me
waiting in the parlor! Says I'm a menace to the
neighborhood."

Holmes laughed. "With those scarred knuckles
and that pug nose, I might have made the same
deduction."

I nodded in agreement. "A bit of soap and water
wouldn't hurt you any, young man."

The boy gushed on to Holmes, "Sir, I've got all
manner of information to report!"

Holmes opened the door and stood aside.

"Then do step in, Wiggins."

Mrs. Hudson had stationed herself just inside,

blocking our passage, her hands clasped before her so tightly, her knuckles shone white.

"Mr. Holmes, you know that I insist on orderliness and respectability on these premises at all times." She scowled at the boy. "I'll not allow street urchins—"

"My apologies, Mrs. Hudson, if master Wiggins in any way offended your sensibilities. But he is not of the idle poor. No indeed. Wiggins is an inspired entrepreneur."

"A what?"

I interjected, "The boy sells newspapers at Waterloo Station."

"Oh."

Wiggins piped up proudly. "Aye, and many's the time me stock run out because I was too good at hawking the latest edition."

Holmes rested a hand on the boy's shoulder.

"Compared to some of the riff-raff who have graced these premises under the veneer of respectability, Master Wiggins may look like a street urchin, but he is, in fact, a most enterprising lad on the first mile of a successful path through life. Is that not that so, Wiggins?"

"I couldn't have put it better meself!"

Mrs. Hudson had gone from clenching her fists to wringing her hands. Her eyes alternated between the boy and Holmes, uncertain of the former, trusting the latter... to a degree.

"Mr. Holmes, you will assume responsibility for him while he's under this roof?"

"Gladly and proudly, as will Doctor Watson."

Caught off guard, I mumbled, "Why yes, of course, certainly," not knowing what sort of mischief this boy was capable of.

"Very well then." Mrs. Hudson sent Wiggins a stern look and wagged a finger in his face. "And you, mind that you walk straight out 'ere you take your leave of Mr. Holmes and Doctor Watson. Don't let me find anything missing."

She about-faced with erect bearing and marched off.

Wiggins sighed. "Thank you, Mr. Holmes. She's a dragon, that old one."

"Indeed, she is." Holmes opened the inside door. "Please, Wiggins. Do come in and deliver your report."

I prepared a drink and lit my cigar. Holmes seated himself and filled his pipe.

I said, "And kindly forgive our landlady. Mrs. Hudson was quite rude to you."

Wiggins made a dismissive gesture.

"Not at all, Doctor. The old dear read me like a book. There's a silver candle holder in the hallway that would fetch me a pretty penny, no questions asked."

Holmes chuckled. He got his pipe going and spoke through a cloud of foul gray smoke.

"What have my Baker Street Irregulars learned thus far?"

"Plenty, Mr. Holmes. You've got to lay low! There's a price on your head. Someone in London wants you dead. Someone real powerful."

"I do hate to disappoint you, Wiggins, but I am aware of that. What about Mr. Wells?"

Wiggins' eyes took on the gleam of a rascal.

"There's the juicy part, guv'nor, and no mistake. I was getting to that part next. The gent, Mr. Wells, he arrived by train not two hours after you put me on the lookout for him."

I interrupted with, "Are you sure it was Wells?"

Wiggins took offense. "Would I be reporting so to the guv'nor if it hadn't been duly reported to me or if I hadn't seen with me own eyes?"

Holmes uncharacteristically chose to calm troubled waters.

"Of course not, Wiggins. Do continue."

I decided to not say anything and absorb what I heard. This case was providing ample material for one of my stories, and I must remain attentive. But as I listened, I promised myself that when Mary and I had children, I'd see to it that none of them ever grew into anything like this scruffy lad.

Wiggins said, "I followed Mr. Wells me own self. Timmy had just got back from getting the word out about that chap Albert, so I set up him peddling papers, and I stuck like glue to your Mr. Wells. Get this. The gent has himself a love nest! A flat near

Cavendish Square." Wiggins recited an address which I jotted down, though I knew Holmes would be committing it to memory. "I did some reconnoitering," the boy continued, "under the guise of knocking on doors looking for work, chores and such, but while all that came of that was an offer to clean a stable--which I passed on quite politely, thank you—I did put together pieces of information."

Holmes said, between puffs on his pipe, "Watson, from the standpoint of pure narrative structure, I do hope that as a writer you're noting how Wiggins' masterfully creates suspense by withholding information."

"Holmes, must you always—"

Wiggins spoke over me, unwilling to yield the floor.

"Gents, here it is straight. Mr. Wells is playing house with a doxy named Danielle, who happens to be trollopin' around behind his back with another bloke! Now, ain't that a pip, I ask you?"

"Do you have a name for this other bloke?"

"They call him Big Stan along the docks. He roughs people up for the moneylenders if they don't pay up on time. That sort of bloke. Mean son and no mistake. Big Stan Auger. He's sweet on Danielle, and they've got a hot thing going. I'm surprised Mr. Wells ain't tumbled to it yet."

"And did you by chance learn where Big Stan might be found when he's not sparking Danielle?"

The scruffy boy drew himself up to his full height.

"Not by chance, Mr. Homes. By skill and persistence, like you taught us."

Holmes said, "Touché," with a fleeting smile.

"Big Stan sops up ale at a dockside pub called The Surly Wench. He has a nasty red scar runs across the bottom of his face, or so I've been told."

"Very good, Wiggins. Most thorough. And what of the missing Albert?"

"Alas, Mr. Holmes, as well as we have this city covered, so far there's not been one sighting of anyone matching that name and description."

"Then we must step up the search. See to it."

"You know I will, guv. I mean to say, yes sir, Mr. Holmes. Soon's I hear anything about Albert, I'll get word straight to you."

"Then off with you. As our American cousins would say, we're burning daylight."

"Yes, sir!"

With an informal but heartfelt salute, Wiggins started for the door with the animated enthusiasm only a boy his age can muster.

The door was opened by Mrs. Hudson.

"Commander Standish and Inspector Lestrade," she announced.

Wiggins darted through the doorway, past them before our new visitors could enter. Next to the Inspector, the portly Commander, who was in uniform, stepped aside for the boy, who halted just outside the flat when he got a look at Lestrade, who was in plainclothes. Wiggins made a sniff-sniffing sound.

"I smell copper."

Mrs. Hudson glared at Holmes.

"There, you see! A disregard for authority! Anti-social behavior! A criminal in the making."

Wiggins said, "Relax, luv. There's better pickings anywhere in this man's town where Sherlock Holmes ain't residing. As for you, Mr. Copper," he added to Lestrade, "don't bother telling Mr. Holmes that there's a shoot-on-sight bounty out on him because that's old news."

He departed. Mrs. Hudson followed him like a shadow.

Lestrade and Standish joined us.

From their formal manner and grim expressions, one did not need to be a Sherlock Holmes to deduce that this was decidedly *not* a social call.

CHAPTER 14

Inspector G. Lestrade of Scotland Yard was a lean, dark-eyed man. He nodded to me.

"Doctor."

"Inspector."

He indicated the Commander.

"This gentleman and I just happened to arrive at the same time."

Holmes performed a proper introduction.

As they shook hands, Standish said, "I've never had the pleasure of making the Inspector's acquaintance, though of course I'm familiar with your name, Lestrade. The newspapers feature you often when you solve those baffling murder cases."

Holmes nodded. "The Inspector's rise through the ranks at Scotland Yard has indeed been remarkable."

What I knew to be Holmes' sarcasm was, apparently and gratefully, lost on both men.

Lestrade said, "Thank you, Mr. Holmes. You see, Commander, it is Mr. Holmes himself who has, er, uh, at times assisted me, shall we say."

"Most impressive," said Standish, "knowing that two such impressive minds can work together."

I made myself another drink. I asked around. Lestrade and Standish declined.

Lestrade was, in fact, a dull-minded, slow-witted, unimaginative bureaucrat whose plodding methods and mentality could resolve only the most cut and dried investigations. Great minds working together? The only reason for Lestrade's rise through the ranks at the Yard was that he called, and often, upon Sherlock Holmes for assistance and advice.

Holmes said, "Have a seat, gentlemen."

Standish said, "Thank you," and claimed an armchair near a low fire in the grate.

Lestrade remained standing.

"Sorry, but I can only spare a minute." He scowled in the direction of the doorway through which young Wiggins had exited. His dark eyes reminded me of a ferret. "And it would seem that the wind has been taken out of my sails, for in fact, I have come by to warn you about the rumor of there being a reward out for your demise. I thought you should know."

"I am much obliged, Inspector."

"I can offer police protection. I can have men assigned—"

"That's very kind but no, thank you. Doctor Watson's presence is sufficient."

I lifted the lapel of my coat. Nappy McGuire's .44 rode comfortably under my left arm in a shoulder holster supplied by Holmes, who had also provided me with a box of ammunition that resided in my pocket.

A frown creased Lestrade's features.

"You know it's against the law to carry a concealed weapon, Doctor."

I said, "Couldn't the same be said for putting a death bounty on a man's head? You offered Holmes protection. Can you refuse me offering him the same, and speak of technicalities if he accepts?"

"Well, since you put it that way, and coming from a man of your class and experience, Doctor, uh, I suppose there's no harm in it." The ferret eyes narrowed. "You wouldn't know, Mr. Holmes, who it is that's put the word out on you?"

"We're looking into that," said Holmes truthfully. "I shall notify you at once, Lestrade, when I acquire information that I think will be of value to you. Thank you for your time and concern."

"Well then, I'll take no more of your time, gentlemen. A pleasure to have met you, Commander."

Standish acknowledged with a nod, "Inspector."

Holmes walked Lestrade to the door.

Lestrade said, "Were it not such a miserable day, and were you not otherwise engaged, Mr. Holmes, I would invite you to accompany me. There's been a disturbance in Leicester Square. I'm headed there now."

"A disturbance?"

"Gunfire. Strange motorized contraptions." The Inspector smirked. "Confidentially, I think we're dealing with a case of mass hysteria and hallucination. Good day, gentlemen."

Holmes closed the door after him.

Standish said, "An uncomfortable coincidence, encountering the Inspector here like this."

I said, "Lestrade will find plenty to keep him busy when he gets to Leicester Square."

"Actually, Doctor, I've dispatched a special squad that I suspect had the Square cleared of debris and that... thing on the roof most likely before you gentlemen traveled from there to here. The initial report I received by telephone of the crash debris and the body were enough for me to link this to what happened at Moriarty's castle. Every trace of what happened at Leicester Square has been cleared away."

"There were eyewitnesses."

Standish nodded. "Good, solid citizens who have been dispersed by my people. The police will hear different versions of what happened, depending on who they talk to, but there's nothing to worry about from a security standpoint. My Department operates with impunity, and for now, this business of zombies and flying machines is being kept strictly under wraps on a need to know basis to avert arousing widespread panic among the populace. It has been deemed at this point that Scotland Yard does not need to know. Good men, every manjack of them, but when it comes to security amongst that many personnel, well, there can be more holes than a sieve."

Holmes returned to his chair. He relit his pipe.

"How much do *you* know, Commander?"

Standish sighed. He closed his eyes and massaged his eyelids with the thumb and fingers of his right hand.

"More than I wish to, and that is God's truth. Doctor, I would trouble you for that drink now that the Inspector has gone. I didn't think it proper for a policeman to see an officer of Her Majesty's service drinking while on duty but, well, a brandy if you have it, please."

"Of course."

I promptly fulfilled his request.

He downed the brandy.

He said, "There is a widely held belief among Her Majesty's military commanders and advisors that when the next war comes, it will be a mechanized war of the modern industrial age."

Holmes said, "The flying machine I took down was equipped with a death ray."

Standish exhaled deeply.

"Before we continue, I must swear both of you to

absolute secrecy. Please do not take offense, as your credentials are beyond reproach, I know. But you do not possess the necessary official clearance. I am, however, in a position to waive that detail."

"You have my word," said Holmes, "as an adviser to the crown and as an Englishman."

I said, "The same for me."

"Thank you both. Well then, it's not pretty. Some damn fool unit, buried so deep in Accounting files that they'll never be traced, until recently had been conducting scientific research, developing invisible gases and serums and the like and, yes, a death ray, for wartime use."

Holmes set aside his pipe.

"How did Moriarty obtain this technology?"

"A woman named Danielle Kurvisa, a civilian worker in a civilian clerical support position attached to the unit. In fact, it was under civilian cover that the experiments were conducted."

"Experiments?"

Standish nodded. "She disappeared with research data and materials that were not discovered missing until after she was gone. Heads rolled, of course, but by then it was too late. My chaps had lost track of her... until today when she's part of an attempt on your life."

Holmes left his armchair. He peered through the rain-bleared window at the street below.

"She's exactly the sort of woman Moriarty would

use. Brilliant. Beautiful. A skilled actress. Yes, the Professor's brand is on her."

Standish said, "Missing with the young lady," said Standish, "was a serum that had only been administered once," he swallowed hard, "with disastrous results."

"What kind of serum?"

"I'm no scientist, and more's the pity since I cannot offer you a scientific answer or even, God help me, an educated one. I only know this. The aim was to develop a super soldier. To greatly enhance the size and abilities of infantrymen for when England finds Herself thrust into a mechanized war. It was never tested on soldiers. For the initial experiment on its effectiveness, denizens of the slums were cheaply recruited. They never returned to their haunts. In their work, little notice was taken. The research was immediately terminated when it was discovered that the serum had, er, unfortunate side effects."

"And what would those side effects be?"

Standish spoke slowly, with obvious reluctance. "Subjects of the serum experiment turned into, well, they turned into zombies. The word zombie is widely misused and misunderstood, but in this case, the terminology is appropriate. The walking dead. Blindly intent on a hideous craving for human flesh. Superhuman. Indestructible. And totally insane, craving only to destroy and devour. And here is the truly shameful and scandalous part that cannot yet be revealed, not even to Scotland Yard. It must be contained until we have full control of the situation. Three of the subjects who were administered the serum committed suicide... but that leaves quite a few unaccounted for."

I gasped. "How could they be unaccounted for? Surely, Commander, they were kept under lock and key—"

"They were abducted from the facility where the experiments were being conducted. Hi-jacked. Whatever the term one uses when zombies have been spirited away. Three guards at the unit were killed by whoever engineered the breakout."

Holmes turned from the window to face us.

"The serum is what Moriarty was trying to interest Count Kleinhart in when we first caught wind of this at Lady Fairfax's party. Moriarty was testing the waters."

I finished the thought. "It wouldn't be beyond the devil to sell that serum to both sides of a conflict."

Standish rose from his chair.

"Gentlemen, I must get back for there is much to be done in the aftermath of what has happened. But I do have one question for you, Holmes."

"Anything, Commander."

"Well... I am obliged to ask why you gentlemen went to The Empire Theater today."

I held my breath, relieved that he had posed the question directly to Holmes and not to me.

Holmes lied blithely.

"Nothing pertinent, Commander. We stopped by for an afternoon libation and some light entertainment."

Standish shrugged as if it weren't important.

"Well then, a fine day to you both. I'm sorry I was not the bearer of gladder tidings. I will keep you informed of any developments."

When we were alone, I said to Holmes, "Do you believe him?"

"About keeping us informed? I would hope so. But then we made the same promise to Lestrade."

"Why your reticence in confiding in them about Wells and the missing Einstein boy?"

"Ah, but what if Albert is missing on purpose, of his own free will?" He lifted an index finger, which he wagged to emphasize the point. "What if Albert does not wish to be found? With Moriarty lurking about, anything is possible."

I said, "The misdeeds of a philandering husband. A criminal mastermind. Futuristic weapons. A mysterious, elusive beauty. Zombies, and now some terrible serum. A missing boy genius..."

He returned to his chair and went about refilling his pipe.

"Watson, are you game for a bit of undercover work? We need to gather intelligence and quickly, in places like The Surly Wench where even my Baker Street Irregulars cannot go unnoticed."

"I don't exactly have an overfull social agenda. And what will you be up to while I am so engaged?"

"Among other things," said Holmes, "I shall endeavor to locate our client. I too remain most curious about Mr. Wells and his time machine."

CHAPTER 15

As a civilian physician, I have brought new life into the world. I have many times seen life slip away before my eyes. But nothing had prepared me for my tours of duty as a field surgeon with a front-line combat regiment in Afghanistan. Combat does things to a man. After my discharge, I became a man with one foot firmly planted in the respectable civilian life of medical practitioner, blessed with a woman who wished only to love and domesticate me and bear my children.

A good life.

And yet...

That other foot was equally rooted in a world of battle and hellfire where the naked sweat of fear and the savage thrill of survival thrived; it had swelled anew within me that night at Castle Moriarty, and those embers had now been reignited.

No wonder Mary and Holmes were so often at

odds, even in their most banal encounters. Each represented my foothold in each of those opposing worlds.

The Surly Wench was a dreary little rat hole on a side street along the waterfront. Low ceiling. Rank with smoke and stale air. An atmosphere of quiet danger. A half-dozen patrons drinking, smoking. A couple of battered wooden tables, each occupied by working men conversing and sharing drinks with women whose frank manner labeled them as members of the world's oldest profession. At either end of a bar sat a man hunched over his drink.

I sat at the bar stool midway between the two men. In the long mirror behind the bar, the reflection of a scar running across the lower face of the man seated several empty stools to my left was clear enough.

I had found Big Stan Auger.

He came as advertised. A muscular fellow of size and proportions similar to Nappy McGuire but with none of Nappy's roughneck good humor. Big Stan had about him an aura of brooding menace.

This was not the first time I had undertaken the role of field investigator for Holmes, and my strategy generally varied depending on circumstance. There are those times when it's best not to draw attention to oneself but rather to blend in and let the information come in piecemeal, overheard in snippets of conversation or in response to subtly phrased, innocent sounding queries. This job called for making things happen that could segue naturally into a conversation with Danielle's boyfriend.

The fact that my appearance was of a more upper-class sort than those around me seemed like something that I could work with.

A surly, moustached bartender wearing a dirty apron took his time about ambling over to me.

"Name it."

I affected my best Etonian accent.

"I believe I'll have a glass of seltzer water. Oh, and kindly add a twist of lemon to take out the bite."

Snickers rippled around the tables behind me.

The bartender sniggered.

"Coming right up, princess."

Movement from my right.

The fellow, seated at the opposite end of the bar from Big Stan, left his bar stool. He ambled in my direction. Not quite as big as Big Stan but just as menacing because he held an ice pick. A foreign cast to his features. Thin pencil moustache. Eyes that held all the warmth of black marble. He swaggered up to stand beside me. Marble eyes glared into my eyes. I don't know what he saw, but I saw the eyes of a cock of the walk who was out to prove to those in this dive exactly what a tough guy he could be, should a stranger have the misfortune of wandering onto his turf.

He said, "You're in the wrong place, mister." He spoke with an accent. He rammed the ice pick into the front of the bar with such force that the blade sank into the wood. "A fancy pants like you might not leave here alive."

Apparently, at this point, I was supposed to shudder into a frightened puddle of gelatin at his feet. Instead, I eased sideways on the bar stool, allowing my coat to part in front so that, just for a moment, he caught sight of the big pistol in its concealed shoulder holster.

The silence around us held that taut razor edge stillness right before violence explodes.

Toffs weren't supposed to pack concealed weapons. The fingers of my right hand lingered near the lapel of my jacket, near the grip of the .44.

I said, "Ice pick against a .44? Get lost, punk."

His nostrils flared.

Was I bluffing? Would I have drawn the gun and scattered the pub with his brains? I had already stuck this gun down the throat of a zombie and blown apart its head. I had that killing edge in me, but of course this lowlife could not know that. He only saw my eyes, and that was enough. Something in my eyes convinced him.

He forgot about his ice pick. He ran away, out of The Surly Wench.

The bartender brought me my seltzer water with its slice of lemon.

The quiet lingered — a softer quiet. Conversations resumed. Street sounds again filtered in.

Big Stan caught my reflection in the mirror.

He said, "That was stupid."

"I beg your pardon?"

"No need. You heard me. That was bloody stupid." His voice was raspy from a lifetime of cigarettes, whiskey and brawls.

"What he did or what I did?"

"Both. What he did was stupid. You carry yourself like a gent what can take care of himself. He shoulda seen that."

"I defended myself. What's stupid about that?"

"He could have friends."

"I'll take my chances."

"And what happened to the Eton accent?"

He had me there.

I'd used the upper crust act for the desired effect--here I was, conversing with Big Stan--so I'd dropped the put-on accent. None too wisely, it now appeared. But I could make this work.

I said, "I wanted to start something. I don't have a lot of time. I'm looking for someone down here on the docks who's connected. I started things rolling, and here you are."

His scarred face turned from the mirror to me study me.

"You're a strange one. What's your story then?"

"My story needn't concern you. The point is that I need to get out of the country, fast."

"Why? Did you kill someone with that gun?"

"Let's put it this way. I'll kill anyone who tries to find out."

"That bad, eh?"

"Can you get me on a ship, preferably one setting sail tonight? It doesn't matter where it's bound."

"They call me Big Stan, by the way."

I waved a hand dismissively. "Names don't matter to me. Can you help me and how much it will cost?"

Conversations around us tapered off. Ears other than mine awaited his reply.

He said, "A respectable looking gent. Travels armed. Knows how to handle himself. Done something so bad he'll kill to keep it from catching up with him." He considered this. "Interesting, and no mistake." Big Stan rose from the barstool. He reached into a pocket and placed a handful of coins upon the bar. "Unfortunately, it's curiosity that drove me to inquire, not any desire to help. So go blow your nose, mate. Pull that gun on me and I'll make you eat it. If you screw up the courage to come looking for me, I'm on the crew of a tug moored at Greenwich Pier."

"I don't want trouble," I said. "I can pay."

Big Stan guffawed.

He said, "Much obliged for the entertainment," and he sauntered out.

I gave him a one minute start, and then followed him.

CHAPTER 16

The tugboat was a two-funneled, powerful looking vessel. Except for the lights that indicated she was moored at Greenwich Pier, in the heart of the waterfront district, the boat was in darkness.

It was not easy tailing Big Stan.

The weather helped, as did the onset of night. The misting dampness turned into fog with an encroaching chill. Few people felt compelled to be out and about on a night like this unless they were working the docks. There were no crowds for me to blend in with as I followed him.

He chose a roundabout route to his destination, no doubt as a precaution in case he was being followed. He looked back several times, but each time the echo of his footfalls would first cease along the narrow, empty streets, and by the time his eyes came around, I was safely ensconced in shadows and fog.

At an adjacent wharf, two barge loads of bricks were being unloaded by flare lights, luminous orbs in the fog. Their vague illumination hardly reached across to where I hugged the deepest shadows.

He boarded the tug. Then he vanished from my sight into the gloom at the base of the tug's wheel-house. A vertical rectangle of yellow light appeared. Big Stan eased sideways through a doorway. The door closed.

What to do next?

I could move in for a closer look. I saw no indication of a posted guard. There was no way of telling how many were aboard the tug. Was Big Stan leading me into a trap? Should I return to Baker Street and report to Holmes? But what if the tug shoved off in my absence?

From behind me, a quavery, phlegmy voice said, "You're not going up against that bunch, are ye?"

The voice startled me, though I tried not to let it show. I turned cautiously.

An old tramp materialized from the gloom. Grizzled. Bearded. Unkempt. The old salt toted a backpack over one frail shoulder. A walking stick was clasped in his gnarled free hand.

I discerned no one save him alone.

"What business would that be of yours?"

I had no wish to be rude, but if something bad was happening aboard that tug, I had little time to spare. But I could not dismiss him outright. An old wharf rat could overhear things. He may already have pieced together the information I sought. *Then a quiver in my subconscious warned me that this encounter might not be as it appeared...*

He pointed with his walking stick.

"You're best off knowing there's man killers aboard that boat. Forewarned is forearmed, young chappie. That's what I always say."

The warning from my subconscious surfaced, becoming a conscious suspicion.

"I suppose you know everything about the crew?"

"That I do and that's a fact. It's Big Stan Auger and his boys. Stan's a tough son and no mistake. The others be just as mean."

The old man lapsed into a spell of hacking and wheezing that concluded with the spitting of a gob of phlegm that arced gracefully over the dockside. His coughing subsided.

I had to laugh.

"Mr. Sherlock Holmes, who do you think you're fooling?"

Holmes was not only a master detective but was also a master of disguise. At various times I have seen him believably disguised as an opium addict, a priest (on several occasions), a vagrant, a murderer, a stable hand and a chimney sweep. He could assume the pallor of sickness, fake seizures, faint convincingly, and imitate deafness, dumbness, and/or blindness. He could adopt a limp in either leg and well knew the dialects, slang, and accents of countless regions.

The tramp snorted. "Mister, you're talking nonsense.

"Holmes, I won't argue with you. You sent me to snoop after Big Stan so you could come down here and conduct your own investigation in disguise."

He peered at me with unabashed curiosity.

"Are ye daft, man? Is that why you're about to board that boat alone? A form of suicide, is it?"

I said, "Enough. Holmes, you have tricked me like this in the past, but I'm not falling for it this time. Kindly drop this charade and tell me what you've learned."

The tramp said, "I'd best be moving on."

He started to shuffle away.

I couldn't help myself. I grabbed his arm above the elbow, gripping bone that felt thin as a broom handle. I wondered how he had managed to fake bone density. It was an impressive disguise.

I said, "Stubborn, eh? I will divest you of this ridiculous disguise!"

I gave his beard a sharp yank, expecting it to free easily in my hand.

The beard held tight.

"Ow! Don't do that! Let me go! I'm not Shamrock Jones, whoever he is!"

He swung at me with his walking stick. I raised a free arm and blocked the stick's weak blow.

The familiar chuckle of Sherlock Holmes drifted out of the darkness from another direction.

"Really, Watson. I've heard that the waterfront is a dangerous place, but I never suspected you of being one of the reasons. For heaven's sake, unhand that poor soul."

Stunned, I released my hold on the beard and the spindly arm.

I managed to say to the old tramp, "Good Heavens! My dear fellow, I am so sorry!"

He snorted. "Take this, my dear fellow."

He swung the walking stick at me again. He missed. The motion caused him to lose his balance. I rushed forward and steadied him so he could retain his balance. He angrily tugged himself away from me. He shuffled off into the night, muttering to himself about lunatics who belonged in an asylum, not out roaming the streets amongst normal people.

My embarrassment gave way to irritation. I looked around. I seemed to be standing alone.

"Dammit, Holmes. Show yourself!"

He emerged from the fog wearing a short-caped coat and his fore-and-aft deerstalker cap against the evening chill.

"Best to lower our voices, Watson." His eyes were on the tugboat. "Sounds carry easily across the water at night."

I lowered my voice. "Damn me for a fool; I was certain that old man was you. What in blazes are you doing here?"

"Apparently saving you from the gallows for the murder of a hapless senior citizen."

I sighed. "Poor fellow. My ire was up. I thought you had again made a fool of me. But I see that this time I did a fine job of achieving that without your help."

He said, "After you left, a telegram was delivered to 221B. It was from the Einstein family in Germany. Mrs. Wells referred them to me. The Einsteins received a letter in today's post demanding ransom for the release of their son. I wired the family that I was already investigating Albert's disappearance, having been retained to do so by Mr. Wells. I assured the family that I would keep them informed of my progress, and of course, I fully intend to do so."

"Any new leads?"

"Yes. An important one. I persuaded my dear to use his authority to gain me the cooperation of the postal service. I learned that the ransom demand was mailed from a post office serving this district. The local postmaster remembered the letter being mailed to Germany by Big Stan."

"Rather unusual for a postal clerk to recall a detail like that, isn't it? They serve hundreds of people every day."

"In this part of town, Big Stan seems to have established a reputation. The clerk knows him by sight and remembered because Stan had never before posted a letter, much less one to another country."

"So Big Stan is holding Albert prisoner."

"The Einstein family thinks so. A lock of the boy's hair and some of his personal items were included in the envelope with the ransom demand. The payoff is supposed to be here in London tomorrow."

"Is the boy being held aboard that tugboat?"

"That's what we're about to find out."

I scanned the fog-shrouded boat.

"Strange there's no sentry."

"There was," said Holmes. "He's presently lying unconscious near the wheelhouse. I waited for Big Stan to arrive before I took out the sentry. I knew you'd be along."

"You knocked out a sentry *after* Stan boarded? I didn't hear a thing."

"My dear fellow, that's because you weren't supposed to hear a thing."

"What about Wells and his time machine?"

"Mister Wells remains unaccounted for, I regret to say, as does his time machine. So, Watson. Shall we what Big Stan is up to?"

I unholstered the .44.

"Let's."

CHAPTER 17

I was first onto the tugboat. The shadow of the bridge took form. A hatchway led below deck. The wheelhouse appeared deserted. A porthole midway along cast a pale oval glow. I held the pistol up, my index finger curled around the trigger.

I sensed more than heard Holmes join me from the deck.

The boat rode gentle swells from the commercial traffic that plied the river despite the fog. The smell of the filthy, oil-streaked water was strong. Water slapped against the pilings. A barge hooted out on the river.

Holmes touched my arm lightly.

He whispered, "Mind your step."

He guided me around a prone figure of the sentry, slumped against the wheelhouse. I would have stumbled if he had not alerted me. Holmes stepped up to the porthole. He risked a cautious glance in, using only the corner of one eye. Then he drew back and motioned for me to take a look.

I did so, discreetly as possible.

The small cabin was a Spartan affair. A spirited poker game was in progress. The air was thick with cigarette smoke. The cabin was littered with empty bottles. Danielle sat at a rough wood table playing cards with Big Stan and a pair of grimy crewmembers.

Dani was presently engaged in raking in her winnings from the previous hand, adding to an already considerable stack of coin and paper. A cigarette bobbed from the corner of her mouth.

"There you be, my laddies. Has the wee thing from the North Country reamed you good and proper?"

One of the crewmen threw down his cards.

"I'm buggered if I ain't flat cleaned out."

Big Stan smirked. "Go topside and relieve Chas."

"Aw, do I have to, Stan? I've lost enough in this game to see who cleans who, ain't I?"

Dani considered the other crewman. "So Alf, are you in or out?"

"Deal me in, Dani."

Dani shuffled and dealt the cards.

"They want to see me clean you out, Big Stan."

"You ain't cleaned me out yet, missy."

They read their cards.

She said, "No, but I'm about to."

Stan groused. "You're a little shark is what you are."

Alf groaned when he read his hand.

Dani chuckled. "Alfie, you need to learn how to play poker." She eyed Stan. "And you keep a civil tongue in your head, lover boy. You're talking to the brains what thought up this caper."

Big Stan read his cards without expression.

"I reckon," he said without expression. "Now shut up and play cards."

I'd seen and heard enough. I eased away from the porthole.

Holmes wordlessly moved on. I kept pace with him. The fog hugged the boat in a damp, vapory caress. Holmes was showing me the layout of the old tug that creaked against its moorings. The Einstein boy was aboard. The kidnappers' security was lax. They were over-confident. We eased around corners, inching along.

Movement!

We halted.

In the weak light, a strange figure emerged from a hatchway. My first impression was of a walking mushroom: a shadowy shape fluffed out at the top, narrowing down, stalk-like; the mushroom image a result of an extravagant, untamed mane of black hair, the length of which bore little respect for current style or convention, topping a thin torso and a skinny set of legs.

The three of us regarded each other in silence for several heartbeats.

Then Holmes said softly, "Mr. Einstein, I presume?"

Teenage eyes held alert wariness.

"Yes, I am Albert." He spoke with a distinct Germanic accent. "You are the police?"

"I am Sherlock Holmes. This is Dr. Watson. We have come to rescue you."

That was good enough for Albert, who said, "I have initiated my own rescue, as you can plainly see. They thought simple knots could restrain me. Ha. My destiny is to unravel the mysteries of time and space. I can untie a knot."

A shout broke the relative quiet of the night.

"He's gone!"

Those around the card table inside the cabin could be heard scrambling to their feet, kicking back chairs.

Holmes said, "This way, Albert."

We started toward the bow.

Danielle was shrieking, "Get them! Kill them, but not the kid! *Do it!*"

Alf materialized from the fog just before we reached the bow, from which it would have been an easy step off the tug. He threw himself at Holmes with the snarl of an angry bear. Holmes met him with a sharp right jab to the jaw. Alf hesitated, shook his head a couple of times and stormed in again. He barreled into Holmes, the velocity of the charge sending both of them off their feet, onto the deck.

I raised my pistol. Holmes would surely throw off his opponent, providing me a clear shot at Alf.

That when Donny, the other crewman, jumped me from behind. The two of us went sprawling across the deck.

Big Stan burst out of a hatchway and went for Albert. He effortlessly hoisted the boy off his feet, into the air.

Donny, having latched onto my back, slammed my face into the deck but I remained aware of Albert's struggling and Big Stan's cursing, and the struggle raging between Holmes and Alf. I rolled onto my side with enough force to throw Donny off my back. He scrambled to grasp the wrist of my gun hand in both of his hands, attempting to wrest the pistol from me.

The gun fired. A sharp, loud report... followed by the *splash!* of someone or something falling into the water.

Had Big Stan, seeing this kidnap job go bad, thrown Albert overboard in an attempt to drown him? Disposal of living evidence, that was the way of the Big Stans of the world.

The thought filled me with renewed energy.

I twisted about again until I was atop Donny. Then I took a chance. I released the pistol. It clunked to the deck. Donny let go of my wrist. He reached for the pistol, exactly as I intended him to. I brought the edges of both hands down sharply upon opposite sides of his neck at twin pressure points.

Donny sagged with a sigh, instantly unconscious.

I shoved him aside. I retrieved the pistol and was back on my feet. I sighed with relief.

Big Stan looked not quite so big in death, sprawled face-down with the back of his head blown away by the wild shot from the .44. Nearby, Holmes rose from having finished off Alf, either permanently or temporarily, I could not discern nor did I much care.

Splashing sounds.

Albert's voice, calm though with what sounded like considerable strain, called to us through the fog.

"I say! I am quite all right, but I require assistance. I do not know how to swim."

Holmes knelt to extend both hands to the young man in the water.

He said to me, "Danielle! Catch her if you can, Watson."

I circled the boat deck, half expecting an ambush. But there was no sign of her.

Danielle had escaped into the fog.

CHAPTER 18

After being fished out of the Thames, Albert dried down in private with an old blanket before donning shabby, dirty workman's clothes that must have belonged to one of the crewmen.

While we waited, Holmes made a fast but thorough search of the cabin, using a magnifying glass drawn from the folds of his coat. He examined what may well have been every square inch, standing on his tiptoes to include nooks and crannies before crawling about on his hands and knees. He rifled through a stack of paperwork.

Then we left with Albert.

I said, "We're leaving behind at least one dead man. The gunshot that killed Big Stan... won't it draw the police?"

"In this section?" was Holmes reply. "Hardly likely." His mouth was a tight line of frustration. "I found nothing but routine paperwork. No clues."

"We found Albert."

Holmes actually patted the lean boy on the back.

"That we have, and for now, that is enough."

Albert's countenance was difficult to read. There was no open show of enthusiasm, relief, or emotion of any sort.

We had to walk some distance before finding a cab stand. Albert looked midway between a wet puppy, what with his hair a scraggly mass flattened against his head, and a child wearing adult clothes, given the baggy looseness of the soiled clothing that drooped from his narrow frame.

The driver we approached looked askance at Albert in his sorry state and then at the two gentlemen who accompanied him.

I tipped the driver generously.

"I am a physician." I nodded in Holmes' direction. "This man is associated with Scotland Yard. We are rescuing this young man from dire circumstances."

Albert stepped forward. He had been shivering when Holmes hoisted him from the filthy river water, but once the shivering passed, a sort of natural decorum returned, considerably at odds with both his youth and his unkempt appearance.

"What the gentleman says is true. You must help us."

That turned it.

Moments later, the driver was snapping his whip

over the head of his horse, and our cab was clip-clopping away from the waterfront.

Holmes said, "Tell us about Danielle."

Albert sighed.

"She's beautiful, isn't she? And really quite intelligent. When Mr. Wells took me to The Empire Theater, he introduced me to her. Her friends call her Dani. After her performance, she joined us at our table."

"Are you aware that Danielle and Wells are romantically involved?"

Albert raised one eyebrow with an air of sophistication beyond his years.

"There did seem to be a familiarity in their interaction with each other that suggested more than a casual friendship. On the Continent, of course, such extramarital liaisons are, how shall I say it, more socially acceptable."

Holmes asked, with a twinkle in his eye, "And so you did not mind cutting in on Mr. Wells by romancing Danielle on your own?"

Albert smiled. "I am shy, yes, but I am not unread in, shall we say, certain areas of human behavior. I am curious about many things. I understand this is normal for a person of my age. I found Danielle's performance and her personality to be most, uh, stimulating. I hardly imagined that my attraction to a beautiful woman could lead to misfortune."

I said, "Believe me, Albert, you aren't the first

man to have *that* thought, and I daresay you won't be the last."

"Nonetheless, it is a lesson I would have preferred not to learn at the price of personal experience. *Herr* Wells made a point, on my initial visit to The Empire Theater, of mentioning to Danielle that I had traveled far from home to meet him. He meant to impress her. He told her that I came from a good family in Germany. Danielle became more interested in me. When *Herr* Wells excused himself to, er, answer the call of nature, I was left alone with Danielle for several minutes."

Holmes said, "I'll wager she found you fascinating."

Albert sighed again. "I realize now it was mere flattery to snare me in a trap. She signed a copy of her picture for me. She told me how interesting I was, a young man my age being so smart and so on. She invited me to return alone and watch her perform with Andre. Well, I returned. I met her after the theater closed." His eyes clouded. "Big Stan was with her, waiting for me. They took me to that boat and held me there until you arrived. Danielle changed. They were not kind to me."

Big Ben's chiming of the nine o'clock hour resonated throughout the London night as the Hansom cab deposited us at 221B Baker Street.

Mrs. Hudson's cry of dismay resonated throughout the house at her first sight of Albert.

"I must say, Mr. Holmes, there has certainly been a flow of, er, unusual traffic through here today."

Holmes was the soul of contriteness.

"Mrs. Hudson, I know this young man's appearance, so soon after the unfortunate performance by our young friend Wiggins—"

I cleared my throat.

"Excuse me, Holmes. *Your* young friend." I caught Mrs. Hudson's eye, which had been alternating between an assessment of the boy's unfortunate condition and her disapproval of Holmes. I said, "Mrs. Hudson, I've always had the greatest respect for your sense of decency."

"And I for yours, Doctor, despite your friendship with Mr. Holmes."

Holmes blinked, genuinely taken aback.

"Mrs. Hudson!"

Her Scottish ire would not be denied.

"I run a respectable house, Mr. Holmes. I wish this domicile to be kept orderly, clean, and tidy. The Good Lord knows that I have tolerated your considerable eccentricities with the best of humor, for I've seen firsthand the good you've done in resolving folks' troubles. But I will not tolerate—"

Albert said, "Excuse me, good lady, but these gentlemen risked their lives tonight to save me from a terrible situation which could have cost me my life."

That stopped Mrs. Hudson. She drew a breath.

"Swear to me on your mother's name that you speak the truth, son."

"I do, for it is the truth. My name is Albert Einstein. Please do not think ill of these men on my account."

Mrs. Hudson considered this.

She said, "I turn to you, Dr. Watson. I know you to be a man of upstanding character; honest and sincerity."

"That is most kind of you to say, Mrs. Hudson. It is as the boy says. He was kidnapped and being held for ransom. Mr. Holmes has been retained to affect his safe return, and that is what we are in the process of doing."

"Your word, Dr. Watson."

"My word, Mrs. Hudson."

"Well then, let us see to young Mr. ... Albert, was it?"

"If you please, ma'am."

Her demeanor warmed.

"Well spoken and well behaved." She stepped forward to place a hand upon his shoulder. "Come, Albert, I will show you where you may draw a hot bath while I find suitable clothing for you."

Holmes said, "It's rather late to find a clothing store open at this hour."

A wee bit of the landlady's frost returned.

"Mr. Holmes, I have not always rented flats to eccentric consulting detectives. I have numbered respectable families among my tenants over the years, and even you would be surprised at what folks leave behind when they move out. I store away what may be reusable, and I believe I will be able to find Albert a fresh set of suitable, dry clothes."

"Of course," mumbled Holmes. "Thank you so much."

Albert sent us a look over his shoulder as he was being led away.

"You will see that my parents are notified?"

"I shall make contact with them at once," Holmes promised.

And so he did, thanks to that new invention, the telephone, which was mounted on a wall of the front hallway. The London Telephone Exchange was only seven years old. Yet, through the wonders of technology, Holmes was able to telephone the telegraph office, where he had established an account and from where the happy news of Albert's rescue could be telegraphed to his anxious, waiting family.

With Albert in Mrs. Hudson's capable care and his business with the telegraph office completed, Holmes struck a match and touched the flame to the bowl of his pipe. His head was soon wreathed by the usual foul-smelling gray cloud.

"So, what do you make of this case, Watson? The damnable thing about the whole affair *is* that I'm quite certain everything that's happening lately *is* connected, but I'm not certain just how."

I said, "As for me, I've grown increasingly disillusioned with Mr. H.G. Wells. Why has he picked such a time to disappear?"

"Perhaps his disappearance was not of his choosing. Or perhaps his lying low is an act of self-preservation."

I pressed on. "And what of this alleged time machine? The very idea is fantastic."

"Some would say the same about zombies. The world is a changing place, Watson. Changing faster than any of us can comprehend. Who can say what the world will be like in, say, 1914? Our military foresees futuristic warfare that can devastate civilization. Let us hope they're wrong. But you deflect my question. What do you make of this business?"

"Sorry. I wish I had something to offer but frankly, Holmes, it seems a rather sticky wicket no matter how one considers it. There are connections. Albert is the houseguest of a married, possibly mad author who claims to have invented a time machine. Albert most likely avoids being seduced by Mrs. Wells only because he's already fallen under the spell of Danielle, who is only setting him up for Big Stan and the kidnap demand. Then this afternoon she's whisked away by Professor Moriarty's minions in their damnable futuristic war machines."

He nodded. "Danielle is the primary connection. She stole the serum. She's Wells' girlfriend. She thought up and implemented the plan to kidnap Albert for ransom."

"So, Moriarty was behind the kidnapping of Albert?"

"No, our dear Professor would never dirty his hands on such a petty crime as kidnapping for ransom. Dani and Big Stan were enterprising small timers. The kidnapping is unrelated to Moriarty."

"What about Andre, the knife thrower?"

Holmes tapped out his pipe bowl into a standing ashtray next to his chair.

"The attempt on my life at the music hall was spontaneous. Dani and Andre had just learned there was a price on my head. When Dani told Andre that I was in the house, he made a try for me."

"But if he was one of Moriarty's people, why was Andre killed on that rooftop while Dani gets whisked away?"

Holmes said, "Moriarty disapproves of his people acting on their own, particularly when it results in failure as did their attempt to collect the reward money that Moriarty himself had placed on my head. Andre was expendable. I suspect that things will not go well for Dani, but Moriarty must yet have a use for her."

There came a polite tapping at our door. The door was opened by Mrs. Hudson.

"Inspector Lestrade."

Holmes promptly rose from his chair.

"My dear Inspector, what a pleasant surprise."

Mrs. Hudson paused with her hand on the door handle. She stood behind Lestrade and sent Holmes a look. Albert would be in his hot bath. Her expression said, *Mr. Holmes, what should I do?*

Lestrade strode in without his usual air of nonchalance.

"My apologies, Holmes, for intruding at this late hour."

"Bosh. Watson and I were just about to leave for a spot of dinner. Would you care to join us?"

This satisfied Mrs. Hudson. She withdrew, closing the door after her.

Lestrade waited until the door latch had clicked.

"I'm afraid this is not a social call, Mr. Holmes, much as I'd like it to be. I must ask you to accompany me. You may join us if you wish, Doctor."

I said, "And what is our destination?"

"The home of Mrs. and Mrs. H.G. Wells. A murder has been committed."

CHAPTER 19

In the front parlor of the Wells home, Lestrade lifted the sheet from the dead face.

Danielle's coloration was already like marble, a mask of surprise and pain. Eyes wide. Mouth a frozen oval. She had been garroted; the length of common household rope twisted tightly around her throat. Her tongue protruded from the corner of her mouth, an obscene thing like a length of rotting sausage.

Lestrade had wasted no time interrogating Holmes. Even before we'd reached Waterloo Station for the train ride to Surrey, he'd said, shortly after leaving our flat for the station, "I came to you directly upon receiving word of the murder. The local constable included in his telephone report to the Yard that the scene of the crime had been recently visited by a Mr. Sherlock Holmes. Mr. Holmes, I'd like to know what your involvement is with the Wells family."

"Sorry, Lestrade. I can't divulge that. It's privileged information."

An irritable snort from Lestrade.

"Well, we'll see about *that*."

Few words passed between the three of us following that exchange.

At Waterloo Station, hurrying to catch our train, we passed Wiggins, who was hawking a late edition of one of the tabloids. He saw us and gave a brief negative shake of his head to indicate that The Baker Street Irregulars had no new word on the whereabouts of H.G. Wells. Neither Holmes nor I acknowledged the boy's unspoken signal. Lestrade proceeded, oblivious to it.

The official activity surrounding the Wells home upon our arrival included uniformed bobbies, police wagons, and one long black coach with government markings drawn up apart from the others, as if waiting.

Inside the little two-story house, through an archway leading from the front parlor, Mrs. Wells could be seen, clad in a bathrobe, seated on the edge of a bed. Hands folded primly in her lap.

Then we were past her, viewing the body. The local constable now stood at parade rest, his hands clasped behind his back, his preliminary investigation officially now in the hands of Scotland Yard. Lestrade replaced the sheet across Danielle's face.

His ferret eyes centered on Holmes.

"The local man tells me that documentation in

this woman's purse indicates that she was an entertainer at The Empire Theater. You already know that, don't you?"

"I beg your pardon, Lestrade?"

"And well you should beg my pardon. When I visited your flat earlier today to warn you about there being a bounty on your head, I told you I was on my way to investigate an uproar in Leicester Square."

"Yes, that is true."

"You and Dr. Watson have previously been guests here in the Wells home, where the woman involved in an attempt on your life now lies dead. I spoke with people who were inside the music hall, so I know about her involvement in the attempt on your life before she fled under, er, uh, unexplainable circumstances. And now she lies at our feet, Dead. What do you know about her?"

"Not very much."

Holmes spoke absently, making a production of studying the placement of Danielle's body in relation to the points of entry into the parlor.

Lestrade said, "You are aware, of course, that it is a crime, punishable by imprisonment, to conceal evidence or in any way hinder or misdirect the police during an investigation."

Holmes said, "A young German national named Albert Einstein is involved. He met Wells through an international scientific correspondence society they both belong to. Albert has been Wells' house guest.

He went missing without taking his belongings with him. Wells retained me to find the boy. Really, Inspector. Have you *ever* found my involvement in one of your cases to be less than advantageous?"

"Well, uh... that's beside the point! I need to determine who's responsible for *this* murder. I would appreciate your cooperation. And quite frankly..." Lestrade paused to nod in the direction of Mrs. Wells, who remained within our line of vision but beyond earshot of our voices. "Mr. Holmes, your assistance interrogating of Mrs. Wells would be most appreciated."

Lestrade, I thought.

First, he accuses Holmes of intruding on his investigation, and then he asks Holmes for his assistance!

CHAPTER 20

We next interviewed Mrs. Wells, who I have referred to as Jane.

Lestrade opened with, "Uh, pardon me, ma'am. It's my duty to ask you some questions."

She raised her eyes, ignoring Lestrade.

"Hullo, Mr. Holmes. Dr. Watson."

"Mrs. Wells," said Holmes.

Recalling her intimate advance during our previous visit, I merely nodded without comment.

Her eyes drifted to the corpse beyond the archway.

"Will they be," she swallowed hard "will they be taking it away soon?"

"Very soon," said Lestrade. "Are you up to a few questions? The constable reports that you found the body."

She said, "I came home from visiting a friend

who's caring for her sick mother. The house was dark, so I knew Herbert was still... that he was not home. I let myself in and when I... when I saw *her* lying there, I ran out of the house. I'm afraid I was screaming. I was hysterical, you see."

I said, "I can prescribe something for you once you've finished here, Mrs. Wells."

"That would be very kind of you, Doctor. I intend to stay with my friend tonight. I couldn't stay here. Inspector, do the police have any idea who did this... and why?"

"Ma'am, I was hoping that you could provide us with that."

"My husband is a teacher and a writer. I am his wife. We do not know people who kill people."

"Forgive me, but I must ask you a routine question. Can the friend you were visiting verify your statement?"

"But of course. Alma and I have been friends since childhood."

"And where might we find Mr. Wells?"

Her eyes dropped to the hands clasped in her lap.

"I don't know."

"Mr. Holmes tells me that a young man named Albert is your house guest."

"Yes, that's true."

"I understand the young man is missing. Or might you know of his present whereabouts?"

"I don't know where Albert is. Why are you

asking me these questions?" Her gaze lifted to meet his. "Do you suspect me of something?"

"Again, Mrs. Wells, these are routine questions. Did you know the victim?"

"No. I've never seen her before in my life."

Holmes said, "Lestrade, I think we should inspect Mr. Wells' study."

Lestrade considered this, along with what little was being gleaned from Mrs. Wells. He nodded.

"Quite so."

They left me alone with Jane Wells.

My first impulse was to accompany them, but something in her eyes bade me to remain, and so I did. She waited until we were alone.

She said, "I owe you an apology, Doctor."

As before with this woman, I felt tongue-tied.

"Er, really, Mrs. Wells—" was the best I could manage.

"Please call me Jane."

"Very well... Jane."

"When you were here last, I behaved wantonly, referring to bedside manner and the rest. I must apologize for embarrassing myself and you."

"Really, Mrs.--that is to say, really, Jane, nothing happened. We must make allowance for the stress you're under."

Damn! It was the wrong thing to say! My comment was intended was to pacify her, but my remark seemed rather to embolden her.

She stepped close to me.

I thought, *Uh-oh!*

She said, "It's just that, well, you're so virile. A woman can perish of loneliness, married to a writer. But I should never have behaved the way I did, for you see," she drew a long pause before saying in a soft voice, after exhaling the long breath, "I am with child."

"Does your husband know?"

"Not yet. Oh, I'm so confused."

And suddenly she was weeping in my arms, her head resting on my shoulder.

I found it extremely uncomfortable. At least we were away from the activity in the parlor where additional official personnel could be heard arriving, entering the house to attend to the removal of the corpse. I'm not sure exactly how long I stood like that with Jane in my arms. The scent of her jasmine perfume caressed my nostrils as before. But I felt nothing resembling desire. Empathy stirred within me.

Eventually, awareness came to both of us. Holmes and Lestrade could be heard returning from their inspection of the study.

Jane disengaged herself from me as if nothing had happened.

Lestrade said, upon their reappearance, "Mrs. Wells, does your husband keep an address book on hand, or any sort of index file of those people with whom he stays in regular contact?"

"Yes, I've seen such an address book. Why do you ask?"

Holmes said, "Most men and women keep their books close at hand wherever they intend to be. There is no trace of any such book or file in your husband's study."

I said, "Wells took the address book with him. He's going to lay low, moving about, staying in contact only with close friends and associates."

Holmes said, "There is the possibility that he was abducted, and the address book was taken with him. But with no sign of a struggle or evidence to point us in that direction, yes, we are left with the reasonable conclusion that Wells has gone to ground. Given the circumstances, there seems to me only one reason that could drive him to such a degree of panic that he would lose his emotional bearings and flee."

Lestrade said, "And what would that reason be, Mr. Holmes?"

"The knowledge that his wife committed murder."

Jane gasped. Her jaw dropped.

"Do you mean to say that you think I murdered that... that *thing* in my parlor?"

"You say you've never seen the victim before. I think you've seen a picture of her. You know who she is."

"You are mistaken, and I have murdered no one."

Lestrade said, "I certainly hope that proves to be the case, ma'am." He sounded sincere.

Jane bristled. "And how could it *not* be the case?"

Holmes said, "A number of items don't add up, Mrs. Wells. Your husband came to me because your house guest has gone missing. Now your husband is missing. And oh yes, there's a murdered woman in your parlor."

"I do not know what happened to Albert, but I can assure you that I have not murdered him."

"In your estimation, who would your husband call upon first to hide him out?"

"I have not the faintest idea as to the present whereabouts of my dear husband. *He* could well be the perpetrator of this crime! I have murdered no one. I am being persecuted in my own home."

Holmes eyed her coolly.

"There was a charged emotional undercurrent coursing through this house, madam. I sensed it on my earlier visit when I found this." He produced the kerchief embroidered with her initials. He handed the kerchief to Lestrade. "This was among Albert's personal effects."

Lestrade's ferret eyes shifted from the kerchief to the woman.

"Were you and this Albert—?" He let the sentence drop midway short of lewd suggestion.

Jane Wells emitted a short moan, remained seated on the edge of the bed, staring at her bare feet.

"I know it looks bad, but my only crime is that I'm going crazy, driven to the brink by the man I love."

Lestrade blinked.

"What the devil?" His eyes swung to me. "Doctor, just now you were alone with Mrs. Wells. What were the two of you were talking about?"

CHAPTER 21

What was I to say?

What was I to do?

As a medical man, I felt compelled, regardless of the circumstance, to honor the woman's request for confidentiality regarding her pregnancy. On the other hand, I would not in good conscience withhold information that could influence an official investigation.

I chose the middle path.

I said, "Mrs. Wells has been under considerable stress. This can often result in erratic, emotional behavior in women as well as in men."

Lestrade hardly took time to consider this.

He said, "Another question, Mrs. Wells. Did Albert snag that kerchief *from* your, er, drawers, or did you place it in the boy's things for him to find?"

Holmes said, "The latter, Inspector. Isn't that so, Jane?"

"Yes." She spoke in a small voice. "I... I was lonely."

Seeing the woman in such a state did tug on my heartstrings.

I said, "There there, Jane. You must calm yourself."

Holmes said, "I'm afraid, Watson, that for Mrs. Wells there is little for her to be tranquil about." His clipped tone razored through my measured cadence. His gaze never left the woman. "Jane Wells is a woman scorned twice over and the reason lies dead in the parlor."

Jane said, after a single, soft sob, "God only knows how the trollop came to be in my home, as she is now."

I said, "Are you saying that you knew of your husband's infidelity?'

"A woman knows, Doctor. Mr. Holmes is right. I found more than one program of Danielle's so-called performances when I once searched my husband's study in his absence. I recognized her from the pictures when I found her. Did Herbert bring the slut here into our home? To think that he would do her... in our own bed." She shuddered as if caught in a draft. "It is as terrible as murder itself."

Lestrade prodded gently, "The kerchief."

"I placed it in a teenage boy's luggage... I can only imagine how pathetic an act that must seem to you, and you're right. I was crazy with jealousy. I was lonely. So dreadfully lonely. But I swear to you, gentlemen, I did not kill that woman. I swear I didn't."

Holmes said, "When you planted the kerchief in Albert's things, you found a signed picture of Dani. Two men, your husband, and Albert, spurned your affections for hers."

Lestrade cleared his throat.

"I'm sorry, Mrs. Wells. Two men are missing. You admit to having been in a lovers' triangle, and the other woman was murdered in your home. I'm afraid I must ask you to accompany me to Scotland Yard."

Jane's desperate eyes swung to me.

"Dr. Watson, surely you can intercede on my behalf." She reached out, vaguely gesturing with both hands. "Please! Tell them I could never do such a thing!"

Empathy again coursed through me.

Then I caught Holmes' direct, dispassionate gaze.

I said, "Jane, it will be best if you accompany the Inspector. You'll be treated fairly."

"You believe I'm guilty too! Everyone believes I killed her!"

We stepped from the bedroom. Holmes drew the drapery across the archway, granting her privacy.

Lestrade was summoned outside by one of his men. He returned a minute later, uncertainty in his eyes.

"The government coach outside. Commander Standish awaits you."

The activity in the street had not diminished. We approached the government coach.

I said, "Er, Holmes, there's something of a rather delicate nature that you should know about regarding Mrs. Wells. It may help to explain her extreme behavior with regards to flirting with me and acting improperly toward Albert. I am betraying a confidence, but I confide in you."

"Then pray do so. How you do prattle on sometimes."

I ignored that and said, "First I would like to state that I simply do not believe Mrs. Wells is capable of strangling another person to death in her own parlor, or anywhere else for that matter."

"Dear me. Watson, have you fallen under her spell?"

"Not a bit of it! I simply don't want to see an innocent woman sent away for something she is incapable of. With everything that's happening—kidnapping, zombies, a time machine, people disappearing—you surely don't honestly believe that poor housewife to be a murderess."

"Not for a minute."

I blinked, momentarily stunned by his reply.

"Then why subject her to more of, well, of Lestrade? For my money, the woman is a victim. I may appreciate H.G. Wells, the writer, but I shan't in the future confuse the man with his art. The fellow is a scoundrel of the first rank, carrying on with Danielle while—"

Holmes completed the sentence for me.

"While Mrs. Wells is in the family way."

"I say, Holmes!"

"Watson, I am always distrustful of what has been erroneously labeled 'the weaker sex.' I am not, however, distrustful of my powers of observation. There is enough about madame's demeanor and behavior, in addition to several physical indicators, for the trained eye to deduce that she is in the early stages of pregnancy. I do not believe Jane Wells to be a murderess. I doubt your friend could slay the proverbial housefly."

"Do you know what's going on, then?"

"I know chess, and I know Moriarty. Now we know what 'further uses' Moriarty had for Dani. She was sent to the Wells home by Moriarty. She followed his instructions because she had no idea what was about to happen to her. She had served her purpose in initially acquiring the serum for Moriarty and romancing Wells. The Professor had her stringing Wells along in an attempt to get his hands on Wells' time machine, and he ordered her to do the same with Albert when the boy showed up. But Dani was too ambitious for her own good. When Moriarty found out about it, she had to be punished. The kidnap and ransoming of Albert without Moriarty's sanction... the Professor couldn't abide that. Danielle had to be made an example of to any of his other subordinates who might be considering a score of their own."

I said, "When she disappeared from that tugboat, Danielle was whisked away by Moriarty's people thinking that she was being rescued as she had been in Leicester Square."

"You've got it, Watson. They brought her here, where she was done in and left for Jane Wells to find. Like the bounty that has been placed on my head, her murder is a move intended to sidetrack and impede us."

I said, "If Danielle was murdered by killers dispatched by Moriarty, why in blazes were you so extraordinarily enthusiastic about Lestrade taking the poor woman into custody?"

"I steered him to her because Jane *is* innocent," said Holmes. "That makes her vulnerable. Lestrade will question her and ultimately release her on her own cognizance, yes, but given the complexity of this case, the safest place for her is in police custody until this is resolved."

I said, "What about Wells as the murderer? Who knows how many times the cad brought Danielle to his house, into the conjugal bed, during his wife's absence? Suppose Dani and he quarreled? They quarreled, and Wells killed her."

"And escaped in his time machine?"

"Holmes, I'm serious."

"Then do forgive me, but we're keeping the Commander waiting. Let's see what surprise he has in store for us. It will not be good news. There is deviltry afoot this night."

CHAPTER 22

"They came from the sky!" screamed the man with the idiot eyes.

A countryman. Sixtyish. Scraggly beard. Rough-hewn. Slack-jawed. Slump-shouldered. A dead, hollow voice.

Holmes said to him, "Tell us everything."

We had accompanied Commander Standish to a government-run lunatic asylum in the heart of London, differentiated from other such institutions by its security measures. Armed guards opened the gate for the Commander's coach. It had been a hurried trip from Woking. We made good time, the official coach charging unhindered along the roads. My friend spoke little during the journey. He was withdrawn, his mental energies turned inward. We had come to this windowless consultation room.

I stood with Standish off to the side.

Holmes sat knee to knee with the wild-eyed fellow.

"They came from the sky!" the man screamed again. "They came with the sun. They live only to kill and destroy!"

Holmes said, "Who are they?"

"Horrible creatures. They kill men, women, and children. The very old. Babies. Gone. All gone. Nothing stops them. Nothing. I saw them rip the intestines out of Mrs. Chetworth! Another pulled Mr. Swain's head off as if plucking a tomato from the vine. Sweet Jesus, protect us! They came from the sky. *They came from the sky!"* His shoulders sagged, chin resting on his chest. He commenced rocking back and forth, arms akimbo, moaning. "They came from the sky..."

I stepped forward.

"Enough. This man needs sedation and rest."

Holmes said, "Quite right. Thank you, Mr. McDill."

McDill said, "They came from the sky," one more time before the orderly led him away humming a tune that had no melody.

The tune seemed to linger after the door closed behind them.

I said, "Poor devil. He's been traumatized, perhaps beyond the point of no return."

Holmes said, "The creatures he spoke of... how like those beasts at Castle Moriarty."

The word came unbidden from in a whisper: "Zombies..."

Commander Standish said, "McDill was one of seventy-six residents of a small crossroad community in Devonshire, a dreary place on the moors that nobody visits unless they have to. Isn't even on the map. Five structures. Utterly remote."

"I know the area," said Holmes. "Unpopulated. Barren. Inhospitable. A brooding place."

"McDill is the only survivor. He somehow managed to escape physical injury, but as you can see, the chap is clearly classifiable as walking wounded."

"What is it precisely that he survived?"

Standish said, "Gentlemen; I can *show* you."

He unsnapped a leather packet he'd brought in from the coach. He withdrew eight-by-ten photographs, which he passed them to us.

I was reminded of the pictures taken by the American photographer, Mathew Brady, of battle-fields of the U.S. Civil War. The art of photography had improved over the intervening thirty years, but the photographs Standish showed us had about them the same grainy, almost out of focus quality as those Brady photographs; the same inhuman carnage and gore, starkly revealed.

The little crossroad community had been photographed in daylight, at various angles, so as to leave no doubt that the area was littered with human remains. Corpses were scattered across the ground, draped upon the steps of buildings where doors had been ripped off hinges and windows broken. There were close-ups of dead men, women, and children. Corpses so horribly mauled that it was impossible to determine their gender. Bodies with decapitated heads. Entrails covered with black spots that at first appeared to be flaws in the picture but, upon closer inspection, proved to be flies. One common denominator united the expression on every dead face, even the decapitated heads upon the ground: a look of sheer horror, greater even than the agony of their grisly demise.

I said, "My God. It's as if demons of superhuman strength and ferocity ran amok."

We handed the photographs back to Standish, who returned them to the leather packet.

Holmes' expression was grave.

"Only Moriarty would dare loose such madness upon the world. There is our evidence. His creatures are the residue of that military experiment. At their deepest core, no matter how dead their minds, there burns within them the impulse to blindly assault and devour."

I asked Standish, "Do we know how many were responsible for this, and where are they now?"

"The situation is being contained under the strictest secrecy," said the Commander. "It's why McDill was brought here. He's in an isolation unit.

He told us there were only three of the creatures. They were found wandering the moor, covered in blood. One was gnawing on a woman's dismembered arm. They were lumbering but deadly. Our chaps actually had to blow them to pieces with artillery. It is only the fact that the area is so remote that news of this has been contained. A delivery wagon happened upon the scene not long after the massacre took place. The driver who reported it is being held in temporary custody to keep him quiet, poor chap. But it would cause mass panic if word got out. It's been determined at the highest level that the general public is not quite ready for reports of zombies terrorizing the populace."

Holmes said, "And what is this about them coming from the sky?"

"The delusions of a man in traumatic shock."

I said, "Perhaps not. We launched our probe of Moriarty's castle from the air. I remember that clearly enough. And so zombies attacking from the air? The possibility is real and frightening. Is there information can you provide that those pictures do not show?"

"Perhaps the most perplexing aspect of all," said Standish. "It was a modest little community, to say the least, but of the several standing structures, each was thoroughly looted of anything remotely of valuable. The community, in other words, was picked clean of valuables."

"Is it possible that local human scavengers descended on the scene after the zombies had left?"

Holmes had tapped tobacco into his pipe. He struck a match and touched it to the bowl. Within moments foul smoke wreathed his thoughtful countenance, making the small room stuffy to an almost unbearable degree.

He said, "Such a scenario might be worthy of consideration were not Moriarty involved. What happened in that remote community was of a dry run, mark my words. A dress rehearsal. Zombies air-dropped and in their wake, a band of highly organized looters, well-trained by Moriarty, who systematically strip a community of all valuables while the zombies cause a diversion."

I waved my hand before my face to clear aware some of the foul smoke.

"Then what remains is location and timing."

Holmes shook his head, no.

"On the contrary. We presently possess that information. It remains only for us to do something about it."

Commander Standish was frowning. "I'm afraid I don't quite follow. Time and location, you say?"

"Consider. The attack on that crossroads was carried out at dawn. That is crucial. It is, in fact, the time when many famous military attacks throughout history have been successfully launched. As to location, is that not obvious given the grand design of this undertaking from the beginning? Gentlemen, horror of an unthinkable magnitude is about to be unleashed unless we can stop it."

Standish glanced at his pocket watch, his forehead pearled with perspiration.

"A zombie attack upon London at dawn? Sweet God in Heaven. That's only two hours from now!"

CHAPTER 23

Mycroft's massive, pasty white, totally naked body executed expert backstrokes along the length of the oversized, rectangular indoor swimming pool.

Holmes and I had been shown in by Mycroft's ancient butler, who hastily withdrew.

Mycroft beamed when he saw us.

"Ah, Dr. Watson! Sherlock! What an unusual surprise at four o'clock in the morning!"

We had parted company with Commander Standish, who would organize and coordinate what response he could to the ominous threat prophesized by Holmes. We'd hired a coach that brought us straightaway to Mycroft's posh home.

Holmes said, "A matter of the utmost urgency has brought about this untimely intrusion, dear brother."

The sight of Mycroft swimming in the nude was not a pretty sight; not unlike observing a whale, ungainly and yet smoothly moving through the water.

Mycroft seemed to penetrate my thoughts.

He said, "Yes, I've read *Moby Dick*, of course. Who hasn't?"

I averted my gaze as if intently infatuated with the multi-colored tiles that enlivened the vaulted ceiling. I heard him emerge from the pool.

He continued, "Melville's best, no doubt, though it certainly could have benefited from judicious editing, wouldn't you say? The fellow does adore his whaling minutiae."

Holmes said, "To business. I've come to avail myself of your office as Her Majesty's Chief of Intelligence."

I took a chance. I glanced in Mycroft's direction. He had (thankfully!) donned a bulky cotton robe that reached to his thick calves. Water puddled at his feet.

He ignored his brother's terseness and addressed me.

"A pleasure to see again, Doctor. You are no doubt familiar with Sherlock's lack of social grace. Let's see. The last time I saw you, you were stepping out of an airborne dirigible. I was gratified to hear that you survived."

We shook hands.

Holmes said, "Please, Mycroft. We are here because I need only to verify a hunch, and everything may then fall into place."

I said, "Indeed, Holmes? Share with us what you've deduced."

"Reasoned would be more accurate, and forgive me, but right now there isn't time. We must work fast to avert disaster. I need the present status of the dirigible, *Blackhawk*."

I said, "We could have asked Standish about that. The airship is under his command."

"I prefer the Commander focus on his agenda while we pursue this."

Mycroft led us deeper into the house. He trailed droplets of water. "Avert a disaster, you say? A matter of life or death, then?"

"More than you can possibly imagine. Quickly, can you determine the *Blackhawk's* present whereabouts and status?"

The living quarters occupied an entire wing and were lavish as befitted a gourmand and *bon vivant*. A manned communications room kept Mycroft in direct contact with the world outside.

We entered his private office, a utilitarian cubicle only large enough to accommodate Mycroft's girth, a wide desk, and a row of filing cabinets. We stood in the doorway and watched him go directly to the nearest filing cabinet. He opened the top drawer and index-fingered his way through the files.

"Here we are. The *Blackhawk*." Mycroft lowered his heft into the swivel chair. He flicked the folder open on his desk, referring to the file inside. "Inactive," he reported.

"Then it's moored at that supposedly inactive industrial complex north of London."

Mycroft further perused the file.

"Right, as usual, Sherlock." He closed the file. "Any other questions?"

"A request. Watson and I are on our way to that airfield. You're aware of the stolen zombie serum?"

Mycroft's eyes tightened.

"I am."

"Moriarty has used it."

"Used it? You mean—"

"He's auctioning off the serum to foreign powers, and he's bred monsters that he's about to turn loose on London, along with a trained army of looters descending in their wake. The airfield is their staging area."

"But why should *you* go there?" said Mycroft. "What If Moriarty is setting a trap for you?"

Holmes chuckled without humor. "I'd be surprised if he wasn't. But I'm the only man in London to match wits with that fiend until a force can be mobilized and dispatched to seize control of the airfield in the face of what is likely to be heavy resistance. Moriarty's looters will be well armed, and the zombies... can be unstoppable."

Mycroft said, "I can't work miracles. A squad of bobbies on such short notice, yes—"

I grimaced. "Our civilian police force wouldn't last a minute. We need the military."

Mycroft said, "I'll contact headquarters and order up troops, but even that will take time."

I couldn't believe hearing my own voice say, "What about your... street friends?"

Holmes nodded. "Mycroft, you must dispatch an agent without delay to Waterloo Station. A newsboy. Wiggins. Inform the boy what Watson and I are up to. Tell him exactly what we're going up against. He'll know what to do. And let us not forget Nappy McGuire."

For Mycroft's benefit, I added, "A bouncer at The Empire Theater in Leicester Square."

Holmes said, "Tell Nappy the same as Wiggins. Stress urgency to both."

Mycroft duly jotted down these instructions.

"The Empire? Those ragamuffin street urchins? Rather an unsavory lot, what?"

"True enough," said Holmes. "But they could be instrumental in saving this blessed city from a hideous fate. Come, Watson. It's time for the showdown with Professor Moriarty."

CHAPTER 24

A forested perimeter surrounded the "deserted" industrial complex.

The hint of a false dawn drew its thin gray line along the eastern horizon, like light escaping from beneath a closed door. Faint city sounds carried from the distance, London awakening to a new day. But in this remote corner of the city, Holmes and I had what remained of the night to ourselves.

We advanced through the forest, guided only by illumination refracted from scudding clouds. We reached a ten-foot-high brick wall. Vague activity could be discerned from somewhere beyond. Tall trees lined the outside of the wall.

I said, "Getting in should be easy enough."

He nodded. "Getting out, on the other hand, could prove to be a sticky wicket. Are you sure you're in this with me all the way, Watson? We are at the point of no return."

I did not dignify that with a response. Without further comment, I started scaling the nearest tree. Holmes matched his actions to mine. We each found a sturdy branch overhanging the wall.

The strangest thought passed through my mind. Here I was, a physician who should be treating patients during the day and enjoying a cozy family life with a fine specimen of womanhood during his leisure hours. Mary had unselfishly given onto me her heart. So what the hell was I doing, climbing over a stone wall with a.44 like a schoolboy at play? And yet the .44 was loaded. And the danger was real.

There was my friendship with Holmes. He and I had taken enemy fire together before and no doubt would again if we survived this. But there was another reason I chose to tread upon this dangerous, unknown ground.

I felt *alive!* Heartbeat pounding in my ears. Excitement racing through my veins. A terrific feeling! I was born a man of action, and I was ready to kick ass.

We made it easily over the brick wall, remaining engulfed in shadows at the inside base of the wall.

Smokestacks towered against the gloomy sky like giant tombstones. There were train tracks, a spur line hosting a row of abandoned coal cars.

And above it all loomed the *Blackhawk!*

The long, ominous shape of the magnificent dirigible was tethered to a tower before the largest of a line of hangars. Hovering there, its black fabric making it almost indistinguishable from the velvet mantle of the night sky, the military's state-of-the-art airship reminded me more than ever of a giant behemoth transported from some far planet or another dimension. Its oversized gondola, at ground level, was blocked from our view by the line of coal cars. Activity buzzed around the dirigible.

A sudden pounding of cadenced boot falls, magnified by the predawn stillness, was coming in our direction! A sentry patrol!

Holmes and I darted toward the nearest coal car. We dodged around it, crouching.

A six-man patrol marched past in military formation, rifles uniformly slung over their shoulders. Their bootfalls seemed deafening as they marched past, within an arm's length of us.

I held my breath. The possibility of being caught and dying with a bullet through my head suddenly lent great appeal to the notion of lying in a warm bed at home, safe with Mary in my arms.

Then the sentries were past, their bootfalls receding.

Holmes nudged me in the ribs with his elbow.

"Break's over. Let's take a look at what's going on and what we can do about it."

We flitted from shadow to shadow. Not possessing my friend's skill in the martial arts, the pistol felt comfortable in my hand. Holmes led us in a direction that I at first thought was taking us away from the airship until I realized that he was bringing us in from their blind side. We crouched behind a small hangar next to the huge one before which the *Blackhawk* hovered.

It was a sight that will be forever engraved upon my memory.

The atmosphere buzzed and clanked with movement. Men were boarding canvas-covered wagons with military precision. My gut tightened with anger. It would make sense for Moriarty to recruit from the ranks of rotten apples who had been kicked out of the service, or perhaps even good soldiers, unemployed and grown restless in civilian society. Either way, the armed men boarding those wagons were no untrained ruffians.

I whispered, "Moriarty's army of looters."

"Counting the drivers, that's at least fifty men. And look, Watson. Over there."

I followed his gaze to the tarmac in front of the main hangar.

"My God..."

A single file line of zombies was filing aboard the airship!

Riflemen stood by while others wielded whips, herding the zombies.

They staggered up the boarding ramp with blank stares. Herky-jerky movements. But not docile. Arms cocked before them. Fingers bent like grasping claws, lusting to destroy. Fiery madness burned in their eyes. The zombie's heads had been uniformly shaved bald so that, wearing shapeless gray garb, it was impossible to distinguish them by gender. They snarled and glared their way aboard the airship.

Meanwhile, the wagons carrying the looters drew into a straight line. The rear flaps were drawn. The wagons, lettered with commercial markings, would not draw attention as they convoyed through the city.

From our concealment, Holmes pointed again.

"There."

Dwarfed by its sheer size, a solitary figure stood before the large hangar, observing.

I uttered his name as a curse.

"Moriarty."

Holmes spoke in a restrained voice. "Now it's up to Nappy and friends and our Baker Street Irregulars. Or we take on this bunch on our own."

"What about Commander Standish? Where is he?"

From behind us, the Commander's voice said, "I'm right here. Freeze, both of you."

A lantern flared on, its brilliant beam pinning us.

We turned carefully, each raising a forearm to shield our eyes from the direct light of the lantern.

Standish stood there with a pistol in one hand, aimed at us, and the lantern in the other.

I confess that it took me a startled moment to comprehend.

I said, "Commander, there must be some mistake--"

Holmes said, "There's no mistake. The Commander is Moriarty's man, and we are now their prisoners."

CHAPTER 25

Holmes raised his hands. I set my pistol on the ground, cursing myself for being caught off-guard. The same response would be racing through Holmes, though we both did a decent enough job of reacting stoically.

The sounds of what we'd been observing—parading zombies and wagonloads of hard-bitten mercenaries--had covered Standish's cat-like approach.

He retrieved my pistol, keeping us pinned in that circle of light from his lantern. He placed his own gun in a holster under his tunic. He maintained enough distance between us so that neither Holmes nor I had sufficient opportunity to rush him.

He said, "Raise your hands too, Dr. Watson. No businesses from either of you or you're dead. Now, *march*. The Professor is expecting you."

I noted a small smile on Holmes' face.

I said, "What in the world can you find amusing at a time like this?"

"Timing, Watson. Timing is everything."

Standish said, "Shut up, both of you."

Moriarty smirked when the four of us grouped beneath the looming *Blackhawk*.

"Ah, my worthy adversary. Holmes, you are a difficult man to kill."

"I should hope so."

"And yet here you are. This time *I* have succeeded, no small thanks to Commander Standish. Per my instructions, he planted the seed tonight that led you here."

"You are persistent; I'll give you that."

I could not help but vent my emotions at Standish, who wore a mild sneer.

I said, "You, sir, are a traitor of the worst stripe. You betrayed your country for *greed*? From one military man to another, Standish, may your soul rot in eternal hellfire." I turned to Holmes, the truth still dawning within me. "When the *Blackhawk* flew us to that assault on Moriarty's castle, Standish was delivering us into a trap, and he knew it."

Moriarty responded before Holmes could:

"That is quite correct. I wanted to witness your death, Holmes. And to yours, Doctor. I owe you both for the times you've thwarted my plans. I knew I would have to deal with the both of you when I learned that you'd picked up the scent of Lady Fairfax's fop nephew who so wanted to be a spy. You would learn of my plans and try to stop me; thus, I chose to avoid that by removing you entirely. You thought you were following clues. You were lured to my castle with the unwitting assistance of dear Count Kleinhart who, you may be interested to know, has been eliminated for his efforts."

Holmes said, "Apparently it's not healthy for foe or friend to associate with you, eh, Professor? At your castle when we proved hard to kill, you countered with a nice touch by instructing Standish to lead a ground charge to our rescue. You sacrificed a few of your death machines, having Standish's crew blow them apart so as to strengthen our faith and trust in him."

Moriarty smiled. "Holmes, I'd sacrifice anything to get you where I have you right now. You and Dr. Watson are not only at my mercy, but you are about to witness one of the most spectacular feats in the history of crime. Commander Standish will glide the Blackhawk silently over London at rooftop level, releasing the zombies, resulting in widespread panic as you can well imagine... and evacuation." Moriarty indicated the line of wagons. "My men will then move in and stack those wagons with everything of value they can carry, after which they will meld into the city amid the panic and confusion. A brilliant plan, is it not?"

"Audacious, though the Commander's villainy comes as no surprise to me."

Standish's sneer grew wider and meaner.

"More deductions from the master detective."

"Not deduction this time," said Holmes. "Reason. Logic. You were involved from the beginning, Commander, and yet with all of the resources at your command, you never seemed to make progress. Your link to Moriarty? Elementary. After Watson and I were involved in that firefight atop The Empire with one of his zombie flying machines, it caused quite a stir in Leicester Square and quite a mess. *You* claimed credit for having *your* men swoop in and clean away the mess even before Inspector Lestrade got there. Reason dictates then that if Moriarty's force was in place and ready to so promptly arrive in their machines to rescue Danielle and try to eliminate us, and your people were simultaneously in place, despite the fact that you claimed they'd lost track of Danielle after the serum first disappeared, it had to be orchestrated. That meant that your people were working with Moriarty's people. You were a part of it. You'd sold out."

I said, "The information Standish supplied us with information, such as Danielle being the one who stole the serum or the attack on the crossroads community, we would have acquired anyway through Mycroft."

Holmes said, "You've got it, Watson. The Commander thus gained our trust and reported our progress to the Professor."

With the zombies aboard the dirigible, the whip-handlers and riflemen started dispersing toward the smaller hangars. Three of the riflemen strode in our direction.

Moriarty said, "I must say, Holmes, you are extremely confident for a man about to die."

"Perhaps I am winning this chess game you're so intent on us playing."

Moriarty laughed. "Chess? Winning? You're about to *die*, Holmes. That is *not* winning. I'm about to order the Commander here to put a bullet through your brilliant head. *That* constitutes winning. Why on earth have you put yourself and Dr. Watson in this position?"

I said, "Uh, not to be contrary, Holmes, but right about now, I'm sort of wondering the same thing."

Holmes said, "Knowing is one thing, but there is no solid evidence to prove what I know to be true. Thus, the only way to *prove* your guilt, Moriarty, is to catch you in the act."

Standish said, "I overheard something about Nappy McGuire and the Baker Street Irregulars."

Moriarty laughed again.

"That scurvy rabble of orphans and a nightclub bouncer? Enough! Commander, I order you to fire a bullet into the head of the great Sherlock Holmes. Do it *now!*"

CHAPTER 26

The knuckle of Standish's trigger finger whitened as he started to squeeze the trigger.

I bunched my muscles, about to hurl myself at him in this last desperate moment.

Then a section of the brick wall, over which Holmes and I had gained entry, blew apart in an explosive thunderclap of brick and mortar! Echoes of the explosion surrendered to the battle cries of howling attackers who swept in through the breach. The assault force had acquired dynamite from some-where and knew how to use it! Nappy McGuire's underworld connections apparently were extensive indeed.

For one second, our attention flickered in that direction.

Except for Holmes!

His right leg swung up, fast. The tip of his boot

struck Standish's wrist with an audible, bone-crunching *snap!*

Standish yelped in pain. The pistol (the .44 that I'd been carrying!) slipped from his fingers and clattered to the ground. Stunned, he could not resist when Holmes swooped in and then swiftly drew back with the Commander's holstered pistol in his hand.

Moriarty shouted at the approaching riflemen. He pointed at us.

"Kill them!"

The riflemen unslung their weapons, tracking them in our direction.

I retrieved the dropped .44. Holmes and I reacted like we'd rehearsed the maneuver, pitching ourselves forward to the ground. I took aim at the rifleman on our right who, like his mates, was caught off-guard and was in the process of tracking his weapon downward. I plugged him twice through the chest. My bullets knocked him off his feet and he did not move. Holmes placed a slug through the forehead of each of the other two.

We picked ourselves up. Dusted ourselves off.

Moriarty and Standish were nowhere to be seen.

The line that tethered the *Blackhawk* to its tower fell away!

The human tide that had blown its way in through the hole in the wall swarmed in while Moriarty's mercenaries poured from the wagons to engage them.

I recognized Nappy, the ugly, redheaded giant from the Empire, at the front of the attackers. To his right stormed freckle-faced, pug-nosed Wiggins. To Nappy's left, little, thin but determined Timmy. Behind them charged dozens of street denizens of every age. Underworld street toughs recruited by Nappy, and just as many young ruffians including Baker Street Irregulars. The hastily assembled assault force was largely unarmed, unlike the mercenaries, yet the attackers had the advantage of total surprise, and a sort of rabid fervor fueling them, descending on the mercenaries with clubs and fists in a melee of hand-to-hand combat.

The massive engines that powered the dirigible hammered, drowning out the sounds of fighting. The ominous, streamlined of the airship became a formidable, almost invisible presence in the remaining pre-dawn gloom of the sky. The engines mounted in the cowlings gave a first burst that initiated forward thrust. Then the pilot shut off the engines.

Holmes snarled like an oracle cursing the gods.

"Moriarty and Standish are likely onboard that airship to oversee their handiwork. They're getting away!"

The silent, gradual withdrawal of the black shape of the zeppelin was a ghost-like sigh that sent shivers down my spine.

Then another sound!

A *whompa!-whompa!whompa!* that I'd heard only

once before when Holmes and I were under attack by Moriarty's death ray flying machine at Leicester Square!

A weird, shiny black metal gyro craft, identical to that one, shot out from one of the small hangars as if fired from a cannon. It quickly lifted to hover over the hand-to-hand fighting that raged around the wagons.

This left, from the direction of another of the hangars:

*Whompa!-whompa-****chug!****-whompa!*

*Whompa!-whompa!-****chug!****-whompa!*

I said, "How many of those machines from hell does Moriarty possess?"

"At least one of them is having problems."

We dashed, fast as our running legs would take us, to the open front of the remaining hangar.

And there it sat. Another of the death ray flying machines. A pilot in the cockpit. His gunner outside the craft, fiddling with piping that led from the steam engine. The fury of the steam engine's racket shook the confines of the hangar.

*Whompa!-whompa!-****chug!****-whompa!*

Then they saw us.

The pilot sprung erect. He held a handgun that spat orange-red flame in our direction. The other man drew a handgun. Holmes and I each fired without slowing. The pilot sat back down. His chin tilted forward onto his chest. The other man pitched onto the ground, lifeless.

I shouted at Holmes, "Now what?"

He crossed to study the piping for perhaps eleven, maybe twelve seconds. Then his nimble fingers, that could coax a concerto from a violin, fiddled there briefly.

The misfiring engine instantly corrected itself.

Whompa!-whompa!-whompa!

Whompa!-whompa!-whompa!

Holmes whipped open the side hatch door. He unceremoniously heaved the dead pilot from the cockpit. With the grace of a gymnast, he flung himself into the cockpit with its wide windscreen that curved around the front of the futuristic contraption. He glanced out at me.

"Coming, Watson?"

CHAPTER 27

Our gyro craft bolted forward the instant I stepped aboard.

I braced myself against its frame with one hand. With the other, I grasped the mounted weapon from which a long muzzle protruded. It was a relief to be on this side of the weapon! I remembered too well dodging its bluish-white death ray.

We zoomed out of the hangar. The ground and everything below seemed to rapidly diminish in size as Holmes piloted us into a steep climb before leveling off with remarkable smoothness.

I saw the hand-to-hand combat being waged below. I realized how little time had passed. I saw Nappy relieving a mercenary of his rifle, and then using the rifle butt to brain the man. Nappy looked like he was having a great time.

The first gyro craft soared in, seemingly unaware of us. Due to the sounds of our steam-powered gunship, I could hear little, but I saw the jagged bolt of lightning that lanced out from the muzzle of the weapon aboard that other machine.

On the ground, a cloud of smoke and nothing else remained where Nappy had stood!

Rage fired my soul. The clanking and hissing of the mighty steam engine powering us made conversation practically impossible, but I must have let out of cry of anguish loud enough for Holmes, in the cockpit, to hear.

He shouted over his shoulder, "I'm going in! Do what damage you can!"

We picked up speed so fast I was nearly tossed from our machine!

I steadied myself with both hands gripping the mounted weapon, planting my feet firmly. I forced my mind to block out the fantastic nature of this. I was no stranger to military combat but... *in the air?!* In flying machines armed with death rays? Fantastic, yet I sensed that this was but a glimpse of warfare in the not too distant future.

The pilot of the other aircraft became aware of our presence. That machine banked away.

Below, a number of mercenaries had sought cover behind their wagons. They started sniping at the attackers. I saw one or two of ours go down, then another. Moriarty's men were well shielded by the wagons.

I saw another sight that tightened my throat. Timmy had sustained a shoulder wound. The boy was not mortally wounded but was unable to do anything but hunker down and try to keep from being shot. Wiggins shielded Timmy with his body and fought valiantly. Then I lost sight of them in the melee.

My fists grasped the controls of the weapon, which were clearly marked. I sighed. I squeezed the trigger. A sustained rattling and crackling sound. A jagged bolt of lightning zapped out from the weapon's muzzle.

The riflemen and the wagons evaporated in puffs of smoke.

Holmes jerked the steering mechanism sharply, again almost tossing me out through the open hatch with the suddenness of our turn.

Another bolt of the deadly bluish-white lighting from the other craft barely missed us. Holmes steadied our craft. The other started to draw away. I sighted along the muzzle of the mounted weapon. I unleashed another silvery flash.

An explosion, a cloud of smoke and the gyro craft no longer existed!

Holmes piloted our aircraft into a stationary hover over the battleground.

Evaporation of the riflemen and the wagon had demoralized the surviving mercenaries. They were fleeing, wanting only to escape.

Wiggins led the survivors of the assault force, chasing Moriarty's men. The boy was urging on the others like a warrior prince born to lead in battle. I saw Timmy, who was being cared for by some of the other Irregulars. They stopped the bleeding and were bandaging his arm. Timmy looked angry and disappointed more than anything else.

The mercenaries made for the main gates leading from the complex. They'd almost reached the gates when those gates were thrust inward by a company of Her Majesty's troopers. Uniforms and bayoneted rifles swarmed in to halt the fleeing in their tracks. I made out a white horse with a portly man astride it, directing the operation like a field marshal on the battlefield.

The stout, commanding figure could only be Mycroft.

I shouted to Holmes, "Your brother did not let us down! Shall we give chase after the *Blackhawk*?"

I was feeling cocky.

"No need," came Holmes' response. "The *Blackhawk* is doubling back to hunt *us!*"

If one may sound calm while shouting, Holmes conveyed that impression over the *whompa!-whompa!-whompa!* that powered our flying machine. Again, we banked sharply, providing me with a new view. What I saw gripped me with awe and terror.

It was as if the world vanished—the dawn, the silhouetted skyline of London, everything—blotted out by the invisible, silent, enormous black mass that was the *Blackhawk*, bearing down silently on us.

I caught the briefest glimpse of men in the lighted control room but could discern only the features of Standish, not of the men with him. I saw the zombies, packed into the anteroom amidship. Wild beasts, pounding at the windows to get out, even as they were airborne. Mindless of anything but the craving to destroy.

Gunfire opened upon us from the *Blackhawk*.

Holmes called to me, "Hang on!"

Our craft lurched, dipping into an evasive maneuver but not fast enough. Our flying machine vibrated wildly. Then... abrupt silence replaced the deafening racket of our engine.

Holmes said, in a conversational voice as if noting a mosquito bite, "We've sustained an engine hit."

He shoved down on a lever below the control panel. In the sudden silence, the blades overhead had flattened. Their autorotation softened our descending glide, though the ground still came veering up at us.

In those fleeting, jumbled seconds before I lost sight of the *Blackhawk*, I returned fire with my weapon. The bluish-white lightning bolt sought out a target that was almost impossible to see... and equally impossible to miss at this range!

The gondola beneath the airship's massive black shape disappeared with a puff of smoke and a loud *Bang!* that sounded peculiarly flat in the open expanse of sky. Then a much louder series of secondary explosion when the engines and gasses of the zeppelin ignited. Fire engulfed the dirigible in a matter of seconds, an angry, vivid fireball of gigantic proportions that plunged earthward.

Holmes was ripping back on the control lever as we continued our gliding descent at gut-wrenching speed until our craft rose upward sharply, almost standing on its tail, arresting the rate of our dive no more than fifty feet from the ground as if a tug wire had been yanked.

We landed with a grinding, skidding screech. The impact knocked me onto my backside. The craft skidded to a stop. I leapt to the ground, joined by Holmes.

The remains of our flying machine were nothing more than a smoking pile of rubble, inconsequential compared to the wreckage of what had once been the proud, majestic airship *Blackhawk*. Roiling flames lifted from the framework of the mighty airship's tail section, a towering torch that seared the sky with garish flame. The frame of the dirigible collapsed upon itself with a great *whoosh!*

Beyond its ruins, near the main gate, Mycroft sat astride his white horse, as commanding a figure as ever, and oversaw the rounding up of the remnants of Moriarty's henchmen. The Baker Street Irregulars and the others could be seen assisting the troopers. I saw Wiggins helping Timmy into the back of an ambulance. Timmy's wound was not serious. He was good hands and would be fine.

I turned to Holmes.

"How on earth did you know how to fly that infernal death machine?"

"I didn't. I made a few quick calculations, correlating the control panel with the craft's construction and my modest grasp of aerodynamics, and that seemed sufficient onto the task."

"I daresay." I was still having a degree of difficulty grasping the reality that I had survived such a hair-raising ordeal. "Incredible, Holmes! Miraculous!"

He turned his back to me, to the wind, to light his Meerschaum pipe.

He said, around his first puff, "Elementary, my dear Watson."

EPILOGUE

"A request, Watson, if you please. I would like you to shoot me."

Holmes wore an embroidered silk smoking jacket. He stood before the fireplace opposite me, a bemused expression animating his features.

It was late afternoon of that same day. I had dropped in for a brief goodbye to my friend before departing London to join Mary and her mother at the seashore. Mycroft had expedited our being processed through bureaucratic channels in the aftermath of the airfield battle.

A pistol lay on the small table next to where I stood.

I said, without irony, "Believe me, Holmes, over the course of our association I have had ample motive, and sufficient opportunity, to shoot you for some of the scrapes you've gotten us into and for those times you've made me look like a complete, gullible fool."

He smiled. "That's it! Work up a head of steam. You've got every right to at least wing me for some unforgivable slight I've subjected you to under the guise of friendship when all I really needed was a lackey to serve as a sounding board."

His words, spoken in a jocular manner, stung nonetheless.

"Really, Holmes! You're exhausted. You need to rest. It's been a trying case, this latest affair."

"Albert... is he on his way?"

"I've just seen off him in a cab with Wiggins, who has promised to see young Mr. Einstein aboard a train to begin his journey home. That is, unless that rascal Wiggins convinces him to stay on and join the Baker Street Irregulars."

"The future of Albert Einstein," said Holmes, "does not include running with London street ruffians. I took the opportunity to engage the lad in an extended dialogue. I admit to jotting down notes."

"So, what is this nonsense about me shooting you?"

"Someone has to. It's an experiment. You're the obvious choice."

"There are live rounds in the gun?"

"Of course. What would be the point of shooting someone with blanks?"

"Well, I'm certainly not going to shoot you."

"I beseech you, Watson. Trust me. Everything

will be okay, as our American cousins are fond of saying."

"Holmes, I'll make you a deal. Tell me what happened to Wells and we'll take it from there."

Holmes sighed with little patience.

"If you insist. Mr. H.G. Wells initiated contact with me. He sent a telegram that was waiting for me when I got home this morning."

"His time machine?"

"A pathetic hoax intended as a rumor he would circulate to draw attention to his upcoming book with the intention of boosting sales. He's come out of hiding. Claims he was holed up in a rented room working on revisions of an article he's working on and had no idea what was going on. And I believe him. Writers, bah! He's returned to his wife, poor woman. Perhaps this unpleasant affair will inspire the fellow to restore his marriage and be a good father. I'm suspect this will elude future biographers and enthusiasts of his life and work, and that of Albert Einstein for that matter. So there! Are you satisfied? I implore you again, Watson. Pick up the pistol next to you and shoot me. More than once would be preferable."

"Moriarty," I said, stalling for time. "He went down with the *Blackhawk?*"

"He did if he was aboard. We saw Commander Standish in the control room, so we know he went down with his ship. But I cannot believe Moriarty is dead until I see physical proof of it."

"At least we thwarted his scheme to sell off the serum, not to mention his scheme to turn zombies loose over London. Those poor souls, zombies we call them, they were victims of Moriarty as much as anyone. But how did Moriarty learn about Wells and Albert in the first place?"

"Moriarty was a member of the same scientific correspondence society they belonged to, under an assumed name of course. I have a contact in the organization who double-checked the enrollment list. His response came in this morning's post. I'm becoming irritated at your reluctance to accommodate me by granting me one simple request. *Now kindly pick up that pistol and shoot me!* What are you waiting for?"

"For you to come to your senses!"

"All right then. We'll try another approach. I mean, you are winded, aren't you, old man? And do not consider "old man" a term of endearment, by the way. You *are* an old man, Watson. You're not in prime physical condition, the way I am. It's why you chose to marry a dowdy woman."

That caught my attention.

"I say, that's my wife you're talking about. I'll ask you to leave Mary out of this."

"Why? Are you going to shoot me if I don't?"

I tried to ignore the fact that my blood was starting to run hot.

"Don't be preposterous."

"Why, what do you mean?" said he. "What could

be wrong with an old friend and confidant speaking the truth? You're married to a middle-aged woman because you could never satisfy a younger, prettier one. Mary is like you. Set in her ways. Generally uninteresting—"

I snapped. The stress of the preceding seventy-two hours had worn my nerves raw. I snarled.

"Shut up, damn your eyes."

I picked up the gun... and threw it at him with all my strength.

The room became filled with the sound of shattering glass.

Holmes vanished into thin air.

I stared at the shards of glass now scattered across the carpet.

Holmes appeared from the direction of his bedroom. He too regarded the scattered shards of glass.

"A mirrored reflector of my own design." He spoke in a calm, rational voice. "The observer can see through it, and yet it catches and reflects primary objects... in this case, myself. A successful experiment, wouldn't you say?"

I said, "Never again let me hear you speak like that about the woman I love. Mary is a—"

Holmes smiled indulgently. He patted me on the arm.

"I know, Watson. A divine specimen of her gender. Kind, devoted, generous, a loving soul who has enriched your life immeasurably by bestowing upon you the grace of her true love. My dear fellow, I had to get you irate enough so we could proceed with the experiment. And it turned out splendidly, wouldn't you say? You were completely fooled! Throughout our entire exchange, you thought that I was standing in front of you, before the fireplace, when in reality I was standing in my room behind you, positioned so that the device caught and projected my reflection, making you think it was me. It would have been better if you'd fired the gun but hurtling it was enough. It works!"

"Holmes, you're impossible."

He knelt and began gathering the scattered shards of the mirror.

"Now help me pick up this mess, will you, before Mrs. Hudson—"

Mrs. Hudson, already aroused by the sound of raised voices and shattering glass, stood in the doorway, not quite sure whether to react with concern or disapproval.

"Mr. Holmes, I heard a terrible row—"

I interrupted the dear lady, edgy after having been tricked.

I said, "Holmes, you are without a doubt the most conceited, most self-absorbed adult it has ever been my displeasure to be associated with."

Mrs. Hudson sighed, "Oh, dear me."

I went on. "I intend to have no further association with you. I belong at Mary's side, and that's where I'm going to stay."

"Of course, dear fellow, of course." His smile was maddeningly solicitous. "But consider. We've also determined that though you may despise me, you don't despise me enough to shoot me. That's something, is it not?"

I gave up even trying to reason with the man.

On my way out, I spoke to him over my shoulder as I passed dear Mrs. Hudson.

"Mark my words, Holmes. It ends here. I intend to start acting like a married man and get on with a respectable life. No more devices. No more adventures. Ever!"

His parting words followed me from the flat.

"We'll see, Watson. We'll see..."

IF YOU LIKED THIS, YOU MIGHT LIKE:

COMBUSTIBLE: A POST-APOCALYPTIC ROAD TRIP

POST-APOCALYPTIC HORROR MEETS THRILLER IN A DYSTOPIAN NIGHTMARE OF FIRE AND ASH.

The world didn't end with a bang or a whimper...it ended with people bursting into flames.

Across the globe, spontaneous human combustion (SHC) is turning ordinary citizens into living infernos. Governments collapse, cities fall silent, and the air itself tastes like ash. Society burns while the lucky few are left to wonder: *When will it be me?*

Sam and Aja were already falling apart before the fires came. Now, trapped in a crumbling apartment and suffocating under the weight of isolation, their love feels just as doomed as the rest of humanity. But when whispers spread of a small Canadian town called Consumption, untouched by the inferno, hope flickers.

Stealing an RV and refusing to leave Aja behind, Sam sets out on a desperate, ash-streaked journey through a burned-out North America. With his best friend in tow and a growing crew of strange, unforgettable survivors, they chase rumors through a landscape warped by horror, madness, and the heat of human combustion.

Perfect for fans of *The Gone-Away World* by Nick Harkaway and *Warm Bodies* by Isaac Marion, *Combustible* is a harrowing, darkly tender exploration of what survives when everything else burns. Will love endure in a world destined to ignite?

AVAILABLE NOW

ABOUT THE AUTHOR

Stephen Mertz was an American fiction author who was best known for his mainstream thrillers and novels of suspense. His work covered a wide variety of styles from paranormal dark suspense (Night Wind and Devil Creek) to historical speculative thrillers (Blood Red Sun) and hardboiled noir (Fade to Tomorrow). Mertz was also a popular lecturer on the craft of writing and has appeared as a guest speaker before writer's groups and at universities.

www.ingramcontent.com/pod-product-compliance
Lightning Source LLC
Chambersburg PA
CBHW020630250626
47154CB00008B/2612